In the middle of her thoughts, his lips touched hers. She hadn't seen it coming, because she'd been too deep in her own misery.

But the splash of heat that hit her instantly as his lips brushed lightly over hers a second time was unmistakable.

"Relax," he whispered, his hand cupping her cheek, tilting her head upward to meet his next assault.

And it was exactly that, a slow brutal assault of each of her senses. His touch was soft, as if she was fragile and he didn't want to break her. When she inhaled—because otherwise she was sure to faint from the breath she wasn't aware she'd been holding—the scent of his cologne wafted through her like the fresh scent of a summer's rainfall. His voice had been a rough whisper that made her nipples go hard. Then his tongue stroked her bottom lip. She hurriedly traced her tongue along that same spot, loving the taste that slightly resembled the pizza they'd just eaten and the beer he'd consumed. That shouldn't have been sexy in the least bit, but it was. Oh damn, damn, damn, it was.

Books by A.C. Arthur

Harlequin Kimani Romance

A.C. ARTHUR

was born and raised in Baltimore, Maryland, where she currently resides with her husband and three children. An active imagination and a love for reading encouraged her to begin writing in high school and she hasn't stopped since.

Working in the legal field for almost thirteen years, she's seen lots of horrific things and longs for the safe haven reading a romance novel brings. Her debut novel, *Object of His Desire*, was written when a picture of an Italian villa sparked the idea of an African-American/Italian hero. Determined to bring a new edge to romance, she continues to develop intriguing plots, sensual love scenes, racy characters and fresh dialogue—thus keeping the readers on their toes!

For all the latest news on A.C. Arthur books, giveaways, appearances and discussions join A.C.'s Book Lounge on Facebook at www.facebook.com/pages/AC-Arthurs-Book-Lounge/140199625996114.

Decadent Dreams

A.C. ARTHUR

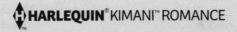
HARLEQUIN® KIMANI™ ROMANCE

To the members of A.C. Arthur's Book Lounge.

Thanks for all your encouragement and support.

Recycling programs
for this product may
not exist in your area.

ISBN-13: 978-0-373-86301-3

DECADENT DREAMS

Printed in U.S.A.

HARLEQUIN®
www.Harlequin.com

Dear Reader,

Sex and chocolate, two all-time favorites! That's the first thought that entered my mind when I heard the title *Decadent Dreams.* The joining of a profitable bakery and a hot and steamy romance was such a great idea I couldn't wait to begin writing!

The elder Draysons have certainly been sprinkled with love. Now, it's time for the grandchildren to find their place within the family bakery business and within a loving and stable relationship. Belinda Drayson-Jones is the epitome of an independent woman, she's gorgeous and wicked-smart and ready to take whatever is thrown her way. Until the man that's been working right beside her turns her whole world upside down. Malik has his work cut out for him in pursuing Belinda, but he's never been known as a quitter.

I hope you enjoy Decadent Dreams as much as I enjoyed writing about the delicious products served at Lillian's Bakery and the delicious nights shared by Malik and Belinda.

Happy reading,

AC

Prologue

Five hundred cupcakes in fifty minutes.

"No problem," had been Belinda Drayson-Jones's immediate response. What else was she going to say? This was her job and she was expected to be perfect at her job as well as everywhere else.

And just to make it interesting, the request was for five different flavors: chocolate-vanilla, classic vanilla, red velvet, triple chocolate and her absolute favorite, dark chocolate vanilla. One hundred of each. Again, no problem.

She'd premixed all her batter so that now it was just a matter of the baking and icing and finishing with crystalized sugar that sparkled with cheerfulness and always went on each cupcake she prepared. It was her signature, one she was more than proud of.

Her kitchen was meticulous, she thought, looking around at the work space on the twelve-foot stainless steel counter. There were three counters lining the baking room of the renowned Lillian's Bakery. Twelve-foot-long shelves—fully stocked with every ingredient they needed for all the recipes prepared at Lillian's—obediently against one wall. Professional ovens on another.

The aroma sifted through the room and her stomach growled but there was no time for food. She only had time to work. "Twenty more minutes," she whispered to herself. The cupcakes were ready to come out. Ten minutes to cool and another ten minutes for icing—and that all boiled down to five hundred cupcakes in fifty minutes.

"No problem," she repeated, slipping on her oven mitts and heading to the ovens.

She took out the first tray so fast she didn't even look at the cupcakes. It was when she pulled out the second tray and turned to place it on the table that she saw the jiggle. One triple chocolate wasn't completely done. Not a problem, she could put back in this tray. She still had time. Except when she reached for the next tray, the vanilla batter wasn't all the way cooked either, because there were big bubbles erupting from each cupcake.

A frown, then a silent curse, and Belinda pulled out another tray to have a closer look. The oven was blazing hot so she knew that wasn't the problem. And before she could give the problem closer scrutiny, there was a popping sound like an explosion, and red velvet batter splattered all over Belinda's face, running down her cheeks and dripping on the black-and-white Betty Boop apron.

A scream bubbled in her throat and died there because Belinda would not succumb to useless reaction. It wasn't her style.

There was a sound behind her and for a quick second Belinda was afraid to turn around. When she did, disregarding that particular emotion she despised almost as much as creamed spinach, it was to see cake batter dripping from every surface in the kitchen. The once pristine countertop she'd been working at was now full of gushing vanilla cake batter. From the supply shelves dark chocolate batter dripped slowly, hitting the floor with a sickening splat.

On instinct Belinda looked at her watch to see the time. Four minutes left.

No prob— She paused before finishing that statement because now the dripping batter was like a hailstorm, the sound loud and resounding, matching the quick pitter-patter of her heart. Her fingers shook; sweat beaded her brow. And then it began, the panic attack that had her bending over quickly trying to catch her breath.

"No. No. No," she repeated over and over, while the scent of cake batter permeated her nose and the sound of loud ticking echoed in her ears. It was a clock and it was ticking down the time. Time, Belinda thought dismally. She was running out of time.

Chapter 1

"Pretty," Belinda said quietly to herself as she stood in front of the flawlessly shined window of Lillian's Bakery.

The legendary upscale bakery occupied half the lower level of a building on Chicago's famed Magnificent Mile, likewise owned by Lillian and Henry Drayson, Belinda's grandparents and two of the most inspiring people in her life. Lillian Reynolds-Drayson had begun testing her baking recipes on the customers of Woolworth's cafeteria in the 1950s back when she was still Lillian Reynolds. Demand quickly grew for her delicious cakes and pies, which was a godsend, as she'd recently become widowed and had a son to take care of on her own. Through her unwavering faith and plenty of elbow grease (as Lillian would advise seriously), she was able to save up enough to rent space and open her own bakery. Eventually Lillian's sweets lured in more than just customers, as she met her second husband, Henry Drayson, in 1960 and went on to have two more children. It was the beginning of a legacy, one Lillian had no idea would be born but now cherished with every breath she took.

And that was the number-one reason that Belinda Drayson-Jones worked as hard as she did. If her grandmother, a woman of small stature but big personality, could build this empire from nothing, then Belinda could certainly do her part to make sure the name and the quality it was known for carried on. Even if it meant losing sleep thanks to that awful five-hundred-cupcakes-in-fifty-minutes nightmare she kept having.

Pretty in Pink was the theme of the front window and it was deliciously gorgeous. White netting lined the bottom of the window while pink confetti sparkled among its sheerness. On white pedestals stood three perfectly decorated wedding cakes, each six tiers. One was pink, the other two white. The pink one had been lavishly decorated with cherry blossoms while one of the white ones displayed perfect blush roses in between each tier. The final white cake was one of her cousin Carter's masterpieces with pink satin ribbons and an intricate lace design that covered the entire cake. It was gorgeous and, since the unveiling of the new window design two weeks ago, they'd already received seven orders for that exact cake, to be made by the fabulous Carter Drayson, of course.

With a satisfied smile Belinda made her way into the bakery, letting the stately and elegant decor—complete with its fresh-cut-flower arrangements that were a must as far as Lillian was concerned—welcome her like a second home. Yes, she could come through the back with the rest of the staff, considering they all parked in the same garage just off North Michigan Avenue, but admiring the window and witnessing passersby as they did the same boosted Belinda's pride and gave her that extra push she needed too much recently.

Amber Mitchell, one of the baker's assistants—who also did double duty as the receptionist when Nichelle, the part-time college student, wasn't in—was standing behind the counter flipping through papers in a loose-leaf binder.

"Twelve deliveries and six pickups today," Belinda told her. "The last delivery is the baby-carriage cake going to Congressman Delaney at his condo, and make sure it stays completely covered. He doesn't want his wife to see it," she said, removing the black tailored jacket she wore with black straight-legged pants and a lavender top.

"You memorize every day's orders, don't you?" Amber asked, her doelike eyes intense with curiosity.

"I like to know what's on the agenda. Keeps us ahead of the game," Belinda told her and received a look she knew well.

It was the look her cousins and most of their staff gave her on a daily basis. The one that said she was taking this business entirely too seriously. It was nothing new and didn't really faze Belinda all that much. Her cousins had always thought she was too serious, too intent on being Miss Perfect. That's what Monica would say. Monica was the younger daughter of Lisa and Dwight—Lillian's eldest son. She had a sister named Shari who was actually the only cousin Belinda could confide in—to the extent that Belinda confided in anybody. As for Carter, he was Uncle Devon's son—Uncle

Devon being the only one of Lillian's children that never married. Belinda's parents were Matt and Daisy, Lillian's only daughter. Belinda's younger brother was Drake. All of Lillian's grandchildren worked at the bakery. As a matter of fact, they should be in the kitchen in exactly twenty minutes for the emergency meeting Lillian had called. Belinda was early. There was no mystery there; she was always punctual.

"I'll get the slips to the back for the delivery guys to look out for," Amber said.

"Is anyone here yet?" she asked, smoothing down her top and making sure there was no lint on her pants. Black picked up everything, but these were her favorite and most comfortable work pants. She had a busy day today so comfort was her first priority. While most of her clothes carried a designer label and made her five-seven frame look even taller, Belinda knew when to sacrifice the look for the feel. In this case the outfit worked both ways, as the pants were designer, an excellent fit, and would still feel comfortable in about twelve hours when she'd finally be able to leave the bakery. And with that in mind, Belinda resisted the urge to find a mirror and double-check the freshly cut edges of her hair or the quality of the honey-blond streaks she'd been adding for the past two years.

"The meeting's not for another twenty minutes," Amber said with a half smile. "You know that nobody is going to arrive until five minutes before."

Belinda sighed. "Punctuality is a virtue."

"More like an obsession where you're concerned," Drake Drayson-Jones said as he entered the bakery.

Before she could turn completely around, he was already leaning forward, placing a quick kiss on her cheek. "Good morning, sunshine," he said with the grin that had won him the Mr. Congeniality award in his high school superlatives.

"Good morning, Drake," Belinda said, shaking her head at her brother, who always seemed to be in a good mood. "You're early. That's a good look for you."

"I want to make sure my presentation is on point, so I had to get here early."

"Presentation? But Grandma called this meeting. I figured that meant she'd do all the talking."

Drake shrugged, heading behind the counter and taking out a Belgian-chocolate frosted doughnut. Before she could remind him that it wasn't even nine o'clock in the morning and he was too old to have doughnuts for breakfast, Drake had bitten through half and chewed it as if he hadn't eaten in days.

"Grandma's going to talk and then I have a few things to say. It'll be short and sweet, I promise."

"But she never calls a meeting on a weekday, in the bakery for that matter. You know how she is about working when in the workplace. What's going on?"

Drake finished off the doughnut then headed to the other side of the showroom where scents of different-flavored coffees brewed at the coffee bar. This convenience had been added to the bakery about three years ago. With the rise of coffeehouses and internet cafés across the nation, Drake was finally able to convince their grandparents to ride the wave. So far, based on how many coffee sales eventually turned into big bakery orders, it was a great idea.

Belinda followed him, taking a seat at one of the four café tables that occupied the space. The quaint little corner not only added ambiance but, thanks to the hand-painted mugs on the tabletops, added a touch of art to the bakery that she loved.

Drake followed her lead and took a seat with his cup of coffee in hand.

"This is a special circumstance," he told her.

"One you are dying to tell me about," she said, letting her hands fall to her lap.

Drake shook his head. He looked a lot like their father with his caramel complexion and thick black eyebrows that matched the soft ebony curls, which he kept cut short.

"Not this time. Grandma wants to make the announcement herself."

"That means it's serious," she said quietly.

"And so are you," he told her, reaching forward to tap her on her forehead. He'd done that since she was little. Belinda half hated it and half loved it because it was a warm memory. Things had changed so much since she'd grown up. "Stop overthinking everything. The meeting will go fine and you'll rise to the occasion like you always do."

He was right. She would. Because that's what everyone expected of her.

Malik Anthony straightened his tie. It was silk and several different shades of blue all swirled into a paisley design. He figured it went well with the dark denim of his jeans and the white dress shirt he'd donned especially for this morning's meeting. Immediately thereafter he had a North Carolina Tar Heels T-shirt he would change into for work because Malik hated ties.

He figured that was one good thing to come out of his departure from the NBA—he didn't have to dress in a suit before and after every game. Now, almost eight years later, Malik could joke about the year he'd played professional basketball. He could look back on that time and not feel a deep sense of loss at a dream long gone. Some would say that was attributed to his laid-back demeanor, that he could always brush off things and move on. They weren't entirely wrong. But he readily admitted that brushing off the NBA was one of the hardest things he'd ever had to do.

Since then he'd found a new career. Becoming a pastry chef had not been on Malik's to-do list. In fact, during their years at college while his best friend, Carter Drayson, had planned to join his family's baking business, Malik had only focused on the fact that Carter always made some banging desserts for their frat parties. Carter would become a businessman, in addition to learning more about the baking craft that had started with him tasting everything that came out of his grandmother's kitchen. He was going to someday either own his family bakery or create his own that would be top-notch because that's the way Carter rolled. As for Malik, it had been all basketball, all the time.

And when that time was gone, he'd had to regroup. Because diving into a pity party for one wasn't his idea of a good time. Instead he'd gone through a year of rigorous rehabilitation, during which time he'd begun taking online courses in, of all things, culinary arts. It was meant as a diversion, to keep his mind off the pain that sometimes threatened his sanity and the loss that could potentially haunt him forever. It wasn't until his therapy was complete that Carter suggested he spend some time at Lillian's Bakery.

Malik had wanted to laugh at the idea of becoming a

delivery man after four years of college, a year playing professional basketball and another year taking online courses. But he needed to do something with his time, needed to keep moving or else he'd stand still in that same place for the rest of his life. So he went to work at Lillian's and eight years later he was still there.

No longer delivering the delectable sweets that came out of this world-renowned bakery, today Malik was a senior pastry chef right alongside the Drayson grandchildren. Hence his dressing up today for this very important meeting with Ms. Lillian, a woman Malik had come to love and respect as if she were his own grandmother.

He'd arrived at the bakery early; then again he did that on most days when he had three cakes to go out by noon. The orders were usually split among the chefs unless the customer requested someone in particular—which mostly happened to Carter, who was as smooth and charismatic as he was the absolute best artisan cake designer Malik knew. While each of the senior team were masters at baking and decorating signature cakes, cookies, brownies and fine pastries, they all had somehow managed to find their own niche that was respected throughout the business. As for Malik, his favorite dessert had always been fresh-baked chocolate chip cookies so it was logical that he spent a lot of time developing new cookie recipes. Brownies were a new specialty that he'd been working on, and after a tremendous response from customers to his new flavors, he figured he'd hit on something big in that department.

There was a children's party later today to celebrate one of the local middle schools' production of *The Wizard of Oz,* so in addition to the three cakes on his schedule, Malik had ten dozen cookies and four dozen mint brownies to bake by three o'clock this afternoon.

He looked at his watch as he moved down the hallway that separated the large kitchen and the offices at Lillian's, and headed toward the showroom. He knew Amber would already be at the front desk since the bakery opened at nine and it was already 8:50 a.m. Now, he would check the display cases to make sure they were full before heading into the meeting—the meeting he hoped didn't take too long.

As he approached the swinging doors to the showroom, Malik heard voices and figured more of the staff was here early this morning. He was just about to enter when he looked through the circular windows first and stopped dead in his tracks.

There should be a law against being so fine and so uptight at the same time. He shook his head as his eyes stayed fixated on her—a pastime he'd long since developed. His body had a systematically physical reaction to seeing Belinda. The heat always started at the top, with a lick of his lips as he swallowed deeply. His chest heaved, his heart rate increasing. Then his fingers clenched because the thought of touching her was almost irresistible. All that pooled into the groin area, causing an undeniable erection. To get rid of it, he'd have to focus extremely hard on something like baseball stats or the last chick flick he'd been forced to watch.

About thirty seconds later his brain would once again take control of his traitorous body and he'd be back to business.

Belinda Drayson-Jones was an extraordinarily beautiful woman. That was a simple fact. Her tall, curvy frame was alluring and the buttery complexion of her skin enticing. But for Malik, it was her eyes that grabbed him by the balls and squeezed so tightly he thought he'd have an aneurysm every time he stared at her. Not just their green color, because he'd seen green-eyed beauties before. No, for him, it was deeper. It was the look of pure sadness that he found in the hazel-flecked depths that kept a stranglehold on him.

Even today, as he finally pushed through the door and walked into the showroom, he could tell she wasn't happy.

"Morning, good people. How are we today?" he asked in his normal upbeat tone as he approached the table where Belinda sat with her brother, Drake.

"Hey, man, glad you're here early. I have something for you," Drake said to Malik as he dug into his leather briefcase and pulled out what looked like a report. "When you get a moment, look that over. I have one for Carter, too. We should meet sometime this week to talk about what we want to do."

Malik took the bound papers from him and flipped through them quickly. He nodded. "That's right. We did talk about this a few weeks ago. I'll look at it tonight."

"When's a good time for you to meet?" Drake asked.

"I'm free this weekend," he told him, still looking at the papers and not at Belinda, who he knew was looking at him.

Here was a fact he'd discovered about Belinda in the years that he'd known her. She had to know everything, be in control of everything and do everything. Now, that seemed like more than one fact, but actually it all culminated into one—perfection. That should have been her middle name. On most days, to the bulk of the people who knew her, it was annoying as hell. To Malik, it was funny and sad at the same time. Some days, he felt as sorry for her as he was attracted to her.

"I'm free for a meeting this weekend, as well," she said in a voice that wasn't husky but wasn't dainty and feminine like her cousin Monica's, either. It was simply Belinda, to which Malik had learned to classify a lot of things about her.

"You're not invited," Drake told her with a quick smile.

"Sorry." Malik added his own smile when she eyed him suspiciously. "No girls allowed."

"Very funny," she said, standing and walking from the table.

Her perfume was heavenly, Euphoria by Calvin Klein. He knew it well and wanted to personally thank Calvin for creating the scent that matched the woman so expertly. He was about to turn and say something else to Belinda when the front door opened and Shari Drayson walked in.

"Grandma's here. Time for the meeting."

Chapter 2

Lillian Reynolds-Drayson walked into the kitchen with an air of royalty that rivaled Queen Elizabeth. She was a tall woman, almost five-seven, with skin the color of warm honey weathered only slightly by time. She wore a rose-colored suit, the skirt modestly five inches below her knee, the jacket custom fit with floral appliqués at the shoulders and down the lapels. She loved pastel colors as much as she loved fresh flowers. But what Lillian loved most was this bakery and her grandchildren, most of whom were assembled around her.

"Good morning. I know you're all wondering why I called you here this morning so I won't beat around the bush," she said.

Lillian stood at the head of the twelve-foot-long stainless steel worktable. To her left, her grandson Drake sat on a stool, his briefcase and paperwork spread out in front of him. Drake always had paperwork because his mind was always busy. That had been the case when he was a child and more so now that he'd grown up and decided he was better at marketing and advertising than he was at baking. After he'd graduated college and come into the fold, he'd brought new-generation fundamentals and visions into Lillian's. He'd been the one to suggest those dang computers that took over most of the duties that Lillian and Henry had done themselves. Not that Lillian was complaining. She knew the day was coming soon that she would no longer stand at the helm of this business, dictating what its next step would be. And she wasn't sad about that. It was the natural course of things. Life had to go on. Together she and Henry had built this legacy so that one day they could sit back and watch their offspring continue on with its success. She'd been fortunate that her grandchildren had the same talent and passion for baking as she did. While her children had also learned at her elbow, watching everything she did, tasting her new creations and helping in the early days of the bakery, they'd all seemed to grow in different directions.

But Lillian wasn't one to be deterred. She knew at some point there would be someone to pass down the bakery to. Sitting right beside Drake was his sister Belinda. A more beautiful child Lillian swore she had never seen. A natural talent in the kitchen, tenacious and unwavering in everything she did. Lillian prayed especially hard, however, over this one every day.

To her right was another one of her granddaughters. Shari was a quiet one, very talented and a great mother to her four-year-old son, Andre. Lillian was proud of how dedicated a mother and a baker Shari had become.

She only wished her granddaughter would one day experience the fulfillment of a good relationship.

Monica was her other granddaughter, but she wouldn't be at today's meeting. Monica had spearheaded one of their newest ventures, the production of dry cake and cookie mixes to be boxed for sale. Today she was meeting with their attorneys and distributors to discuss how to get Lillian's gourmet mixes onto the shelves in as many stores as possible.

Standing beside Shari was a young man who was like a grandson to Lillian. She was the first to admit that she'd initially had doubts about Malik Anthony when he had no choice but to make a complete U-turn from a sports career to delivering cakes and pies all over Chicago. But Henry had convinced her to give the boy a chance. Her dear sweet husband had seen something in this young man that Lillian wasn't quite sure was there. However, over time Malik had definitely proven himself to her and to this business.

She had another grandson, Carter, who was mysteriously missing from this meeting. That fact she would definitely deal with later.

"As you might know already, Daisy just returned from Los Angeles, where she had a meeting with a television studio."

Malik stood up from his seat, going over to help Lillian. Taking her elbow, he guided her down as she angled for the stool behind her.

"Thank you, son," she said with a smile.

Drake was also moving, bringing her a mug that Lillian knew would be filled with her favorite hazelnut coffee—three creams, one sugar. These boys had been raised right and would one day make some woman very happy.

"Daisy attended on behalf of the bakery. When she called me to report that the meeting had been successful, I was beside myself. Henry and I are very excited about this opportunity." As she spoke, Lillian was careful to look around the table at the faces of the people who helped make this a renowned bakery.

In the back of her mind she knew that these bright and talented individuals would need more to draw from than just their undeniable talent for baking, a pretty face or charismatic personality. This was a big opportunity for them, and Lillian only prayed they would be able to come together to pull it off.

"One of those reality TV shows that your generation loves to watch has offered us a place in their next competition, I believe they call it…" she said, looking over at Drake for his input.

Drake nodded and pulled out of his briefcase a couple pamphlets that he passed among his sister, his cousin and Malik.

"*You Take the Cake* is the Festival of Foods channel's highest-rated baking competition. It airs live weekly and features four bakeries that go head-to-head in a cake baking competition. The prize is one-hundred-thousand dollars and national recognition. We're slated to compete in the next competition, which is two months from now," Drake said, barely containing his excitement.

"Are you serious?" Shari asked first as she looked up from the pamphlet to Drake.

"Daisy was very serious about this deal," Lillian answered. "As am I. I hope you all know how important this is."

She heard Belinda sigh as she read Drake's meticulous outline of the details of the competition. He paid as much attention to the details of his marketing presentations as Belinda did to everything else, whether it was baking or simply getting dressed. That girl needed everything to be just right. She'd been that way since she was little, and Lillian had watched her coordinate all the books on her shelf in alphabetical order then make sure each book was lined precisely so that none were sticking out farther than the others. Belinda had even played neatly, keeping all the clothes from her Barbie dolls stored in labeled ziplock bags. And when she packed them away, she was careful to smooth down the hair of each doll before laying them in the box and closing it. Then she would carry the box ever-so-slowly before slipping it under her bed. While Drake's room usually looked like a hurricane had swept through it, Belinda's, even at seven years old, looked as if she'd hired a maid to come in and clean it. The last time Lillian had been to Belinda's apartment, she noted her granddaughter's ways hadn't changed over the years.

"So we're going to compete with another bakery on a national television series?" Belinda asked.

Drake smiled. "Yes, that's exactly what we're going to do. And we're going to win this competition because once we do, Lillian's will be recognized as Chicago's number-one bakery."

"We're already Chicago's number-one bakery," Shari added.

"But this will make us official," Drake told her.

"This will make us national," Malik spoke up finally. "With the win under our belt, Monica won't have any problem getting the stores to carry the mixes. We could open another location, branch out to have shops in different states."

"Now you see where I'm going with this," Drake said. "This is a phenomenal opportunity for us. Once we win, we'll be golden!" Drake told them, unable to contain his enthusiasm.

Even Belinda had smiled at that. "Winning would be a coup for us. We've already been featured in a couple cooking magazines but with this we're liable to make the cover. And Festival of Foods has a great national following. They're the top food channel out there."

"We could try some new recipes," Shari said, tapping her fingers on the pamphlet as she talked. "Do something nobody has ever done before. Different flavors and fillings."

Belinda nodded. "You're right. We need to think about designs, too. Those shows pay a lot of attention to detail. Do we know what the theme is?" she asked.

Drake's smile widened. "Around the World. We've got five different countries to work with. Five unique opportunities to show why we're the best."

"And since we are the best, we're going to wow those judges with our cakes!" Shari added, her excitement showing in the smile on her round face.

"Not so fast," Lillian interjected. "You all are rushing into this like winning is the only possible outcome."

"It's called confidence, Grandma," Drake added, still smiling.

"The same confidence the Hare had when he thought he was a shoo-in to win that race against the Tortoise," she replied with a frown. "Just because we bake good cakes here inside this bakery doesn't mean we'll be able to do the same thing in another location, against other bakers. Talent is not enough for this competition."

"We're not trying to be overconfident, Grandma," Shari said. "We just know what our strengths are. We know what we're capable of because we had the best teacher."

Lillian could have smiled at that compliment but she didn't want her grandchildren to become complacent. She hadn't gotten this far in this business by believing she was the best; she'd done it by *showing* she was the best. Not just in baking, but in customer service and professionalism. This had been no easy feat, and she wanted her grandchildren to realize that.

"And that's why I'm going to teach you something else," she told her grandchildren. "This competition can only be won if you all work together. Teamwork has got to be the key. If all of you go out there trying to show that you personally are the best, you'll fall flat on your face."

"We know that we're a team, Grandma," Belinda added.

Lillian shook her head. Belinda came from what Lillian liked to call "Team Me." She believed that she was the best at everything and so she rarely let anyone help her. She was independent to the point of being a loner and that definitely was not going to work.

"Then it's time you all showed it. Play your strengths and divide and conquer. I want the team to win, not one of you. Your grandfather and I are looking to retire and we'd like to know who's able to run this company and who's not," she said pointedly, being sure to look at each and every one of them that was there.

"We get it, Grandma," Drake said after a moment of silence.

Shari nodded and reached out to touch Lillian's hand. "We'll make you proud."

"I'm already proud," Lillian said.

"Do you know who our competition is?" Malik asked Drake.

"They're all listed in the back of the pamphlet. Two of them are relatively new but one—" He stopped to look up at Shari.

She had just flipped to the back of the pamphlet and they all knew the second she read the list of names because she dropped the pamphlet.

"I can beat her," Shari said defiantly.

By "her" she was referring to Dina English, owner and head pastry chef at Brown Sugar Bakery.

"This is not the place for personal grudges," Drake told Shari.

She lifted her chin and took a deep breath. "I don't hold grudges."

Everyone in the room went silent. That was one of the biggest and most blatant lies they'd ever heard. Shari indeed held a grudge against her once-best-friend Dina English, who had not only branched out and started her own bakery, but had taken a few of Lillian's baking secrets with her. For years Dina had been like a member of the Drayson family, working summers in the bakery while she and Shari had attended college together. When she started Brown Sugar Bakery, it had come as a complete surprise, especially to Shari.

"I mean it. I'll be fine," Shari told them.

Lillian simply nodded toward her granddaughter, hoping she would be able to stand true to her word.

Chapter 3

She'd changed to flat black shoes with thick rubber soles that would grip the floor so there would be no slipping and falling. Her jacket and top had also been changed to a short-sleeved black T-shirt with the word *DIVA* scrawled across her delectable breasts in white rhinestones.

Malik continued to watch as Belinda went directly to the third hook on the rack that held their coats and jackets or whatever else they decided to hang up on any given day. Her apron was always on this hook and nothing was on the two hooks surrounding it. Belinda had a thing about her apron touching street clothes so nobody hung their stuff near hers. She pulled the apron over her head, reaching behind her back to tie it in place. He smiled each time he saw her put that on, he couldn't help it.

"What are you laughing at?" she asked, her brows immediately wrinkling with a frown.

"You," he replied, moving from where he'd been standing across the room to the double Sub-Zero refrigerator.

"I wasn't aware I looked that funny," was her cool retort.

Malik almost laughed again but knew better. There was only so far you could push Belinda and he wasn't trying to get on her bad side. It wasn't quite noon yet so they had a lot of hours to work together in the kitchen.

Shari was traveling with a delivery of two cakes that replicated sculptures by an up-and-coming artist that were being shown at a gallery in Bridgeport. Drake had closed himself in his office, making more moves where the bakery was concerned, no doubt. He was definitely dedicated to the business. As were the rest of the Draysons. They were a close-knit family, the business holding them as strong as their familial bond.

That left him and Belinda in the kitchen today to get out the orders. Carter was expected, but there was no exact time one could ever expect Carter. He worked his own hours, which were usually long and rigorous since he was always striving to achieve more, even though he was already a master at his craft.

"You don't look funny," he said when he'd closed the refrigerator, carrying the rolls of fondant over to the working table. "You look really cute in your Betty Boop apron." It was an honest assessment, one he usually kept to himself. Today, however, Malik had the urge to go out on a limb.

"It was a gift," she said, slapping her hands down over the apron. Too hard to be an attempt at wiping something off, more likely she thought she could erase Betty Boop's voluptuously shaped body from the material.

"A very nice gift. Who gave it to you?" he asked as he worked.

Belinda had finally stopped touching the apron and obviously decided to get to work herself. There were two full sheet cakes on the other end of the table. She picked up a bowl of buttercream icing and a spatula and moved closer to the table, on the opposite side from Malik.

"My father."

"You a Betty Boop fan?"

"Yes."

It was cordial conversation, the likes of which he and Belinda had gone through on more than one occasion. It wasn't normally this stiff, even though Belinda was not a fan of conversing while she was working. But Malik sensed there was something bothering her today. She was even more reserved than normal.

He retrieved a marble cutting board and rolled out the first layer of pea-green fondant. Using the rolling pin, he began the painstaking process of smoothing it out just another layer or so before he would drape it over the golf course cake he was working on.

"I can like Betty Boop if I want to. I'm not so stuck-up that I don't know a simple cartoon character when it's splattered on the front of my apron," she said abruptly.

Malik had looked up at her, not speaking for a moment. She hadn't even gazed at him, just kept scooping icing onto that spatula and gently smoothing it onto the cake. It was amazing how much pent-up emotion she was holding on to. He could see it in the stiffness of her shoulders, the stern set of her lips. And yet, her hands were supersteady, smoothing icing in lengthy strokes, making sure the cake was covered evenly.

"You can like whatever you want. That makes you decisive, not stuck-up." And yet he wondered who'd called her stuck-up, and if they'd had the guts to do so to her face.

"Right," she said slapping the spatula into the icing bowl. She turned the cake, surveying it.

"If you tell me who, I'll gladly punch the person who called you stuck-up," he offered with a serious face. "Providing it's not a female."

The edge of her lips twitched and he knew she wanted to smile. He'd seen her smile before, had received a sucker punch to his gut each time. This one, albeit small, was hard earned. Something was really bothering her.

"It's not worth it," she said with a shrug of her shoulders. "His loss."

The last was spoken in a softer tone. So much so Malik had barely heard it. After only a few minutes of trying to phrase his question just right, he asked, "So a guy you were dating called you stuck-up. Why? Because you weren't into him?"

She'd been making sure the tip was properly attached to the tube and had just been about to apply the border to the cake when she paused. Her head turned to the side and she looked at him. Even on Belinda the white hair caps they were required to wear at all times in the kitchen looked cute.

"How did you know it was a man?"

"Because you're not the type of female to get bothered by what another female says about you. Besides, if it were a female, you would have simply cursed her out and kept it moving."

She chuckled. "You're right about that."

He'd seen Belinda tear down jealous females with a look and a few words spoken in the coolest voice. She wasn't the screaming and hollering type, nor was she into physical altercations. But she was no doormat, either. Anybody coming at her with smart words should prepare to get an earful. So it had to be a man that had said this to her. A dumb-ass man that most likely needed an eye-opener to see the error of his ways. Malik would be more than happy to open his eye for him—or close it permanently.

"It's nothing. Just another date gone wrong. I should probably start my own reality show. Surely my love life is entertaining at best."

Her love life. How long had Malik been thinking about Belinda's love life? Too damned long. Belinda Drayson-Jones was not on the list of available women for him—no matter how attracted to her he was. How attracted to her he had been for some time now. But pursuing her would go against too many of his rules on dating, namely the no-drama rule. If he went after Belinda, Carter would totally go off. The men in this family were very protective of their women. And as his best friend, Carter would definitely have strong feelings about a relationship between Malik and Belinda—especially with Carter's never-mix-work-with-pleasure rule. And then there was the fact that Belinda was Lillian's favorite granddaughter. No secret there. The matriarch doted on everything Belinda did, because everything she did was always right.

Still, he couldn't stop himself from saying, "You're dating the wrong guys."

"Tell me about it," was her reply.

"Okay, I will." He smiled to keep things on this light tone. "Just because he comes from a good family, with money and stature, has a high-paying job and drives a fancy car doesn't mean he should be a candidate."

"That is not how I select my dates."

Malik gave her a knowing look. "You're not going to date any man you think will tarnish the Drayson family name. So in your mind the man for you has to be influential, accomplished, handsome and debonair. Those are all superficial traits, flimsy as the society pages that describe him that way. Hence, big mistake for you."

"Malik, really? Do you think I select men from the society pages? You make me sound desperate."

"Not at all," he said shaking his head. "You're too beautiful to be desperate."

Now, that was a first. Malik wasn't shy when it came to women; he'd just been careful to stay in his lane where Belinda was concerned. With that comment he'd just swerved into the left lane and had to regain his control to keep from crashing.

"That's sort of what he said. Apparently I'm also too beautiful to be so stuck-up."

"Like I said, he's an idiot. Which means you made a bad choice."

"Apparently beauty has nothing to do with that that, huh?" she asked.

Malik wanted to let this conversation drop. He'd never talked to Belinda about the men in her life before. Actually, he'd made a point *not* to discuss that with her. Pity parties weren't his thing so thinking about the woman he'd never had was a pastime he tried to do without.

She'd finished the yellow border of the cake and was just about to line up the previously made sugar roses when one of them slipped from her spatula and landed on the table instead of the cake. She cursed, her lips drawn tightly as she retrieved the rose that hadn't been harmed and put it in its place.

"What you need to do is relax," he told her. "Take some time to just let loose. You'll forget about what's-his-name taking his frustrations out on you." *And you can stop being perfect for just one minute,* he added, though he kept that part to himself. Because Malik was sure the perfect routine was one tiring job.

"I don't see how relaxing is going to make a difference in the man I choose to go out with."

"I'm not saying it'll make a difference in your choice of men, only you can make that change. But sometimes it's good to just get away from all the pressures of life. How about this? I pick you up tonight at seven. We'll go out and have a fun-filled evening at which time you will not think about what's-his-name that didn't have the good sense God gave him. You will not think about this bakery and what orders we have for tomorrow. You will not think about the competition that's coming up or what you can do to contribute for us to win. Deal?"

First of all, Malik Anthony had always been too damned fine for his own good. As if it wasn't enough that his body was perfectly toned, tall and sculpted like the basketball player he used to be. No, his honey-colored skin had to be smooth and enticing. His always-close-shaved head and dark brown eyes were like dangling a carrot in front of every female rabbit. The tattoos he had on each of his biceps should have been a turnoff and yet Belinda had always found the scorpion on his left bicep, which represented his zodiac sign, as well as the justice scales on his right bicep, which represented his mother's zodiac sign, heartwarming instead of offensive.

His laid-back demeanor and almost-always-positive mood tended to give her a headache more often than not. Nobody could be in a good mood all the time. It just wasn't possible. Life wasn't that good. Especially not for him, Belinda presumed. Having his dream collapse and ending up here could not have been easy for Malik. But watching him move around this bakery, laughing and joking with Carter and working just as hard as the rest of them, she couldn't tell he was suffering. Sure, it had been years and he'd probably gotten over the cruel hand fate had dealt him, but Belinda was positive he harbored some resentful feelings. He had to, right?

"I can't go on a date with you. Besides we both have to be back here first thing tomorrow morning. We have a heavy schedule," she told him matter-of-factly.

"We're not the only staff members that work here. Besides, I'm not talking about keeping you out overnight. We're just going to go out for a few hours and have a little fun."

"I don't need you to show me how to have fun," she said defiantly.

"I didn't say I was going to show you. I said we'll have some fun. Meaning both of us. Stop analyzing it to death. I'll pick you up at seven."

"What if I say no?"

"You can. I'm not desperate either, you know. I won't

beg to take you out," Malik said in that casual tone of his.

Why did that hurt her feelings? She didn't care if Malik didn't want to take her out. Why should she?

Rolling her shoulders, Belinda took a deep breath. This was silly. Malik was like family—even though his wide smile and infectious laugh often did things to her that neither Carter's nor Drake's ever had. Spending an evening with him wouldn't be that big of a deal. She'd done it before when they'd worked late nights, or at family dinners. There was no reason to expect that tonight would be any different. And yes, she could use a reprieve.

Earlier this week when she'd gone out with Patrick Masterson of Masterson Wholesale Foods, she hadn't been relaxed at all. And by the end of the evening she'd been ready to wrap her hands around Patrick's scrawny little neck and squeeze until the shrill sound of his voice stopped completely. He was an annoying, self-centered man who thought the sun rose and set on him. And he had the audacity to call her stuck-up because she'd declined a third date.

The first date had been a favor to her mother, who was on some committee with Patrick's mother. The second time had been because she feared she hadn't given him a fair shot the first go-round. After an hour and a half on Monday night and hearing about Patrick's latest accomplishments which centered around his new shipment of veggie burgers and other organic meats, she'd deduced that a third date would be the type of torture she did not deserve.

"I know you're not desperate, Malik." She took another deep breath and used the inside of her arm to wipe her forehead. "You can pick me up tonight at seven. We'll go out and have some fun, because you think that'll make everything in my world better. And we'll be back here tomorrow for work as usual."

Malik looked as if he were going to say something else. Instead he only nodded and continued to work on applying the fondant to the lower layer of the Ricardo wedding cake.

Hours later after they'd both worked themselves to the brink, Belinda drove herself back to her apartment. She stripped out of her work clothes, switched on the faucet in the tub and poured in a generous amount of bubble bath. She couldn't wait to sink down into the water. Heading into her bedroom she grabbed a book from her nightstand. These were Belinda's only indulgences—hot baths and reading. They were her only support system in a life she feared was spiraling out of control.

Just as she was almost out of the bedroom, the phone rang and she circled back to the nightstand to grab the cordless device. She said hello, continuing on her trek into the bathroom.

"I didn't get a chance to ask when I saw you earlier. How was your date with Patrick?" Shari asked. The preschool had called Shari earlier this afternoon and she'd had to leave straight from her delivery to pick up Andre. So Belinda hadn't seen her since this morning's meeting. Of course she thought about her cousin's reaction to the contest announcement—more aptly about how Shari really felt about Dina English and this upcoming competition. Shari had said she was fine with it, but Belinda hadn't believed her. The grudge between Shari and Dina had been going on for years now, but as far as Belinda knew, neither of the women had ever confronted each other or had any reason to be in the same place at the same time. A live competition on national TV probably wasn't the best setting for a reunion, but there wasn't much they could do about that now.

"It wasn't worth talking about this morning and it's definitely not worth talking about now," was Belinda's reply to Shari's question.

"But you two look so good together," Shari said excitedly. "And just think, if you hook up with him, we could probably be a featured bakery in their store. You know those warehouse stores get lots of traffic. They usually make and sell their own baked goods. But what if we could work out some type of distribution with them? We could use that publicity."

This was only a small sample of the pressure Belinda always felt weighing on her shoulders. Ever since she could walk and talk, expectations of her had been high. In elementary school she had to be the cutest, the smartest. By middle school her parents had encouraged—she wouldn't say "forced," out of respect—her to join the spelling club, which had her traveling for nationwide competitions. At the same time she needed to be well-rounded, so three years in gymnastics and four years of piano lessons were also prescribed. High school was the Debate Club, the Honor Society and every honors class she could enroll in. College was more committees and activities, but by that time, Belinda had begun to tune out more than she absorbed.

"You sound more and more like Drake every day," she said. "I'm not going to pimp myself out, even for the sake of making Lillian's a household name."

"Come on, you know I would never suggest that, girl.

I was just saying that would be a perk. Of course you would have to feel something for him, as well. Which by the sound of your voice I'm guessing you do not."

"Then you would be guessing correctly," Belinda said as she sank down into the tub, loving the soothing feel of hot water as it touched her skin, and the chamomile fragrance of the bubbles that permeated the air.

"He's a pompous ass. And he had the audacity to call me names when I said I wouldn't go out with him again. How childish." Even though Belinda had to admit the fact that she was still bothered by his words probably spoke volumes about her own maturity. It wasn't as if she had never been called names before—that, too, had happened when she was younger. Being perfect had never been Belinda's goal—it was a prerequisite. For so long she went along with it because for the most part it came naturally. Now, twenty-six years later, she felt like she was renting space inside this body—living the life others expected her to live. It was a huge price to pay, one Belinda wasn't sure she could continue to afford.

On the other hand, there was the guilt of wanting to lead what she presumed was a "normal" life. Her grandmother had risen above what was expected of a normal African-American single mother, and she'd made something bigger—her family and her business. And Belinda owed it to her, to their legacy, to be the best always. That's what her parents had instilled in her and that was the rule she'd lived by all her life. The one that haunted her to this day.

"So you're on the hunt again?" Shari asked with a chuckle.

"I'm not now, nor have I ever been on the hunt. My

parents are the ones who think I should be married and ready to have babies by now."

"You should have started young like I did," Shari quipped.

Shari was a single mother and proud of it. She took care of her son on her own and never complained.

"I don't even know if I want kids. Or a man for that matter."

"Oh, you want a man," she said. "It's in our genes to want to get married and have kids. We've got a legacy to carry on. If we don't have kids, who does it carry on to?"

Belinda was so tired of hearing about this legacy.

"The show will go on no matter what," she said drily. "Anyway I won't have time to think about men with this competition coming up."

"I know. I've been drawing sketches all afternoon. Andre has a fever so he's been sleeping. But I have so many ideas."

Belinda had none. Sure, Malik thought she was thinking about the competition all day today, and she'd let him think along those lines. But it just wasn't true. This competition was important, she knew that. But there was something else she thought was just as important. Something she feared she'd gone too long without experiencing.

Even now talking to her cousin was a distraction. Belinda had decided to make a change, one that was going to require some thought and planning. "Well, I just came home and I'm trying to take a bath. How about I call you later?"

"Sure, you go ahead. I want to work on my ideas

some more. At some point all of us need to get together to figure out what our game plan is."

Belinda nodded, knowing that would inevitably happen, no matter how much she dreaded it. "Right. You coordinate the others and I'll be there."

"Okay. I'll let you know."

"Hope Andre feels better," Belinda said before bidding her cousin good-night and hanging up the phone.

She lay back in the tub and closed her eyes. She could get out of this tub and climb right into her bed. Sleep would be a good way to get things off her mind—if she could sleep. Most likely she'd continue to think about her life-altering decision—the one she'd made after her date with Patrick. The one where she decided to take charge of her own life. Unfortunately, once again, her life would have to wait. Tonight she had a date. Or maybe she should just call it an outing. Whatever it was, it was going to take her away from planning and contemplating. And Belinda wasn't happy about that.

Chapter 4

"Roller-skating? Are you serious?" Belinda asked when they pulled up in front of the skating rink.

Malik had picked her up in his black Mustang—which had always struck her as too much car for his mild-mannered persona. His personality actually hadn't matched that of the egotistical NBA players she'd heard about, either. He seemed to be different at every turn.

"What's wrong with roller-skating?"

"Nothing," she said with a huff. "If you're sixteen."

He laughed. "Grown-ups roller-skate all the time. Ever watched the Roller Derby?"

She turned to him giving her "not funny" glare. "I'm not wearing gold lamé hot pants or knee-length tube socks. Which further proves this isn't a good idea."

"So you have watched the Roller Derby. I would have never guessed that about you," he told her.

Those words, while they mimicked what she'd been

thinking about him, made her a little more agitated than she figured she was supposed to be on this night of relaxation. Before she could say another word, Malik had gotten out of the car and was on his way around to the passenger side. He opened the door and leaned in so that his face was about five inches away from hers—which for the record was too damned close.

"You'll have fun. Trust me," he said, his lips spreading into a smile. A smile that caused a tugging between her legs.

Despite her inner doubts Belinda stepped out of the car. "I'm really not dressed for this," she said once more.

She wore True Religion leggings and four-inch gray suede platform pumps with a gray tank top that had a scooped neck that gathered and fell like a waterfall. The jeans may have worked but everything else was clearly overdressed.

"You'll be fine," he said, going around to the trunk and popping it open. "I bought you these since I figured you didn't have any."

He pulled out a brand-new pair of white roller skates with hot pink wheels and a stopper.

"You don't know what size I wear," she said. Of all the things men, or anyone for that matter, had given her, skates would have never crossed her mind.

He took a few steps closer to her, closing the gap between them and definitely invading her personal space. "I've known you for almost eight years. I know you wear a size eight pants and medium shirt because your breasts are…fantastic."

She swallowed hard. No, it was more like a gulp.

He lifted his free hand and tucked her hair back behind her ear. "I know that your natural hair color is dark brown, your eyes are green like the sea and your favorite cartoon character is Betty Boop. Even though your father sort of gave that one away."

"Aah, I don't know what I'm supposed to say to that," she replied honestly. How, why did he know all that about her?

"You say, 'Okay, you're right. We're going to have fun.' It's easy."

But it wasn't easy, or at least Belinda wasn't finding it easy. This wasn't a date, she told herself again. Malik was not the kind of man she dated.

Why?

She refused to answer that.

She took a deep breath and exhaled. "Okay, you're right. We're going to have fun."

"That's a girl," he said, tweaking her nose then letting his hand slip down her arm to grab hold of her hand.

Belinda did everything right. She even looked pretty when she cried. Malik remembered her great-uncle Frank's funeral, where she'd sat in the second row right behind her parents and cried softly, a tissue in her hand as she dabbed her eyes. Her makeup had remained flawless, her body still—unlike others who were bent over making a screeching sound. And she wore jeans like no other female he'd ever met. Her smile was gorgeous, her teeth completely straight, her eyebrows elegantly arched. There was nothing out of order with Belinda. Absolutely no faults that could be seen at first sight.

But she couldn't roller-skate worth a damn.

They had gone around the rink one complete time in the twenty minutes they'd been there. Music played loudly around them, something fast with a strong beat that had the other skaters swaying and dancing as they moved around the rink in quick succession. Malik kept them upright, his arms firmly around Belinda's waist as he moved at a slower pace, allowing her to get used to the skates and the people whizzing past them.

"I told you this was a bad idea."

"Nonsense, you're getting the hang of it," he told her. It wasn't exactly a lie. She was no longer gripping his arm as if her life depended on it. As a matter of fact, now that the song changed to something a little slower, she relaxed a bit and focused on moving her legs in the exact motion that his went. After another few minutes they developed a comfortable, albeit still slow, stroll that took them around the ring once more.

"See, you're getting it," he told her with a reassuring smile.

"I guess you can tell this is not something that I do often," she said with her own nervous chuckle.

"I'd be happy to bring you back again. I'm sure you'll just continue to improve."

"I'm sure you're right. Practice definitely makes perfect," she said, this time without the chuckle.

Another circle around and Malik led Belinda off the floor. It took another few minutes to find an empty table where they could sit and be alone. It was Friday night and it appeared everyone had the same idea to spend it at the skating rink. He ushered her to a chair and held her elbows as she sat down.

After a chuckle she said, "Thanks." She was still smiling.

Malik took that as a good sign. Maybe she was having a nice time with him after all. He took a seat at the table opposite her and said, "I would offer to get you a slice of pizza and soda but the food here sucks."

"Thank you for the warning." She looked around for a few seconds as if searching for someone she might know. Then to his surprise she sat back against the chair and drummed her fingers on the table matching the beat of the song that played.

"You know this song?" he asked with what he was sure was a startled look on his face. It was rap music and not necessarily something he pictured Belinda listening to, or daresay dancing to.

"Yes, I know this song. I happen to listen to a lot of music. While rap is not high on my favorites list, I can usually get into a Drake song here and there."

Admittedly intrigued, Malik pressed on with the conversation. "So what other music do you enjoy listening to?"

"I like a little of this and a little of that. R&B, country, some pop and rap, but not too much."

"Okay, so who is your favorite female singer?"

She didn't even blink. "Whitney Houston hands down," was her matter-of-fact reply. Her voice held a tone that said she was ready should he have the nerve to dispute that.

Instead Malik smiled and nodded. "Okay, okay, so you know good music. Now what about your favorite male singer?"

"Solo or with a group?" she asked, seemingly enjoying the conversation.

"Oh, let's live dangerously. Give me an answer for both."

"Solo, Luther Vandross. I have to take it back old-school again and say New Edition and Dru Hill."

Malik couldn't help but laugh at that. Those entertainers certainly were old-school for their age group, but still had a lot of relevance today. "So do you dance, I mean when you're listening to all this music?"

"I've got rhythm, if that's what you're asking. And why do you ask? Do I look like I'm too stuck-up to dance?"

That question effectively sobered the moment. "You don't strike me as the type of person to let someone else's words get to her. Yet all day long you've been preoccupied over what this guy said. Why is that?"

"You're right, this is ridiculous. I'm much stronger than that. And besides, I can easily get another man since I'm so beautiful and so perfect."

Even through the loud music, the sarcasm in that response did not escape Malik. "For the record, that's not what I said."

"But I'm sure it's what you were thinking. It's what everyone thinks of me."

Malik took a moment to think about what he would say next. He'd learned long ago not to act impulsively. Whether it was on the court or with a woman, the same rule applied.

Belinda added, "That's not all there is to me, you know? I'm much more than people see or than the reputation that precedes me."

Malik nodded, proud to hear her say those words. "I believe you. Every now and then, I'm privileged enough to see that you're more than your reputation purports you to be."

She nodded. "I'm glad you can see that."

Now it was his turn to nod. "You don't have to keep

that part of you a secret. It's okay to be who you are all the time."

She was already shaking her head negatively. "I thought you'd been around my family long enough to know better. Obviously not if you think what you just said is true."

"So is your family what's stopping you from being yourself? Is that what you want me to believe?"

"There are expectations in my family for each one of us separately and for us as a whole. Because our parents aren't as active in the bakery business as my grandmother would have liked, my cousins and I were secretly named the dream team upon our birth. Haven't you ever wondered why all of us decided to become bakers?"

Malik resisted the urge to shrug. He had wondered, but hadn't spent a lot of time on it. People had different dreams and those dreams led them in different directions. He should be an authority on that whole subject. "I thought it was a dream that stemmed from the natural talents passed down from Ms. Lillian," was his reply.

"That's what each of our biographies says. A little more eloquently, perhaps." She lifted her elbows and rested them on the table. "But they're just words."

"So becoming a baker was not your dream?"

"I didn't say that," she replied adamantly. "I enjoy working in the bakery. I did inherit a natural talent for it and I'm very interested in the future of Lillian's."

"But?"

She inhaled deeply. Now, that was new. He'd never seen Belinda with what almost looked like defeat on her face.

"But nothing. It is what it is. Are we going to skate some more?"

Malik almost smiled. The calm, cool and always collected Belinda had ended the conversation. And judging by her tone, she informed him that it was not open for discussion again. He stood, taking her arm, waiting while she got her bearings. And as they rolled out onto the floor, once more her focus shifted to moving her feet correctly and holding only his hand. But for Malik, the conversation was far from over.

He had not been wrong when he'd surmised that there was much more to Belinda Drayson-Jones than met the eye. Now that he'd seemingly cracked a little of her shell, his curiosity would not let him back down. Regardless of the ramifications he might face.

By the time they arrived at the pizza place, it was a little after ten in the evening. As this was a very popular restaurant, there was still a good crowd of customers. Luckily, Malik was able to get them a booth toward the back and out of the way of most of the noise.

"So, listen. I know this might not be the fancy restaurant you're used to dining at, but I promise you'll love Giordano's pizza. It's the best in Chicago and I know you like pizza."

"I've had Giordano's before. I was born in Chicago, remember."

"Right," he said with a smile and they both settled in their seats, picking up the menus.

"But you're not from here, are you?" she asked.

He shook his head. "I was born in Philadelphia."

"And you met our dear Carter in college," she said with a slight smile.

"Carter's a good guy," he replied. Belinda knew he was Malik's best friend and the closest thing he had to family in this world. That's why Malik had moved here after his injury. There'd been no place else for him to go.

"He's a great guy, with lots of potential," she said. "I'm very proud of him."

"And he's very proud of you."

She nodded. Nodding kept her from saying something she was sure she wouldn't be able to take back. Something along the lines of, "I need your hands on me again."

Belinda shifted in the seat, the faux leather making a very unpleasant sound as she did. Luckily, Malik didn't look up from his menu or comment in any way. Still, there was something going on that Belinda wasn't a hundred percent sure of. It had started when he'd helped her out of the car. No, before that. When he'd pulled up in front of her apartment building and stepped out of the car. All he'd needed was background music, something with bass that might be heard in a strip club. Not that she'd ever been in a strip club to hear such music.

It was the way his long, lean body had emerged from the car and the way he'd folded his arms over a chest she hadn't realized was so toned and muscled. He wore simple jeans and a T-shirt, an outfit she saw him in daily so it shouldn't have sparked anything different inside her. But it did. As she'd walked down the sidewalk to meet him at the car, she'd felt a tingling begin in the pit of her stomach. That tingling had only increased during their ride to the skating rink because his cologne seemed stronger than usual, more intoxicating. He'd driven with the air-conditioning on so she didn't have the pleasure of a breeze to serve as a slight reprieve.

Then when he'd held her close so she wouldn't fall on her face, Belinda thought she'd melt right in his arms. Instead she had to apply some type of focus because— despite popular belief—she wasn't good at everything. Her legs hadn't liked the fact that she'd put wheels beneath them and expected them to move around agilely. By the time they'd left the skating rink, every nerve in her body was on end and she tingled all over.

Belinda was no fool—inexperienced maybe—but not a fool when it came to the physicality of men and women. She knew the buzz of attraction the same way she knew her mother's recipe for pineapple upside-down cake by heart. She knew it because she'd been feeling it a lot lately. Or rather, she'd been feeling the need to explore other options in the past weeks.

These feelings had precipitated her decision that her life needed to change. There was definitely something lacking in all of her achievements, a void that she was trying to figure out how to fill. For as proud as everyone was of her, Belinda wanted to break the mold they'd cast her in so badly she could scream.

"Chicago-style or thin crust?"

Belinda cleared her throat to cover up the fact she'd been thinking of something other than ordering from the menu. With her cheeks flushed from her thoughts, she closed the menu and sat back against the seat. "Chicago, of course."

"I like shrimp."

She nodded. "And pepperoni."

"Ham and pineapple," he added.

She shook her head. "No pineapple. This is dinner not dessert. I cannot do fruit and meats together."

He laughed at that. "Right."

The waiter came and they ordered the pizza along with a soda for her and a beer for Malik.

She couldn't help but stare at the veins in his arm, which shot upward like taut strands of rope, fading out into the massive bulge that was his bicep. Her mouth watered and she picked up her glass of soda.

"So what do you think about the competition?" she asked after she figured she'd drank enough to either cause a brain freeze or quench her thirst. The former was much more likely since every time she looked at Malik she felt parched.

He'd just taken a sip of his beer and licked his lips as if to savor every bit of the taste. She found herself wanting to also savor the taste…of him. It was crazy, she knew. Malik was not the type of man she normally dated. But he was apparently the type of man to make everything that was "normal" about her raise up and take notice.

"You're looking at me like you've never seen me before," he said out of the blue.

For a second she thought about denying it, but games and lies really weren't her forte.

"Just realizing that things aren't always what they seem."

He nodded. "Things or people?"

"Both."

"So which one of us is different than you thought?"

Good question, she surmised.

"I'd say you aren't what I thought and I'm not what you think. Does that put us on even ground?"

"It definitely puts us somewhere."

Dinner passed with polite conversation, which led to Malik ordering another beer and her having another soda. They bypassed dessert. Working in a bakery all day sort of diminished the taste for sweets prepared by someone else. At least for Belinda it did. She figured Malik was simply being polite.

On the ride to her apartment, Belinda warred back and forth with herself. There was something lacking in her personal life, something that had been lacking for too long to remember. She was a grown woman and her experience was… Well, *next to none* would be accurate. *Virgin* would be politically correct. *Nervous* would carry some truth. And *absolutely tired of all of the above* would be pure unadulterated honesty.

For too long she'd done everything that was expected of her, and with whom it was expected. She'd baked and gone to school and smiled when she was told, danced when it was appropriate, been the mediator when it was required. Everything she'd done in her life had been to someone else's tune. She thought it might be time to make her own music.

"I don't want to be Little Miss Perfect anymore," she said abruptly.

If Malik had been surprised, he didn't show it. He'd simply pulled his car into the parking garage beneath her building. Earlier he'd picked her up out front. She figured—with him being just as protective as her brother and cousins—he'd most likely want to walk her to the door this time and there was no street parking in front of her building.

When the car was parked, he shut off the engine and undid his seat belt. Turning slightly in his seat he looked over at her.

"Then who do you want to be? The CEO of Lillian's? Head pastry chef? The face of the company?"

Each of his questions was condescending to the point where she could feel herself becoming offended. "I wasn't talking about work."

"Oh. So you don't want to be the socialite girlfriend. Arm candy to the next congressman or possibly senator? You want a normal life, a family, the white picket fence, two kids and a dog?"

Okay, now she was officially offended. She should have known better. Why she'd thought Malik could be the one to talk to about this, the one to...

"Fine. I guess you already know everything about me. So I'll just be going," she said, reaching for the door handle.

He grabbed her arm, stopping her retreat.

"I know that you're too beautiful for your own good and that you're used to getting your way. I just want to make sure you know which way you're heading right now."

Sparks of heat soared through her body from the point where his hand connected with her skin, creating a firework effect exploding all over. The interior of the car seemed fifty degrees hotter than it had been before, and suddenly Belinda couldn't breathe.

"Since you know so much, why don't you tell me?" She tossed those words at him as sort of a dare...for herself.

If he made a move, she would follow. Then if it was a mistake it wouldn't be hers.

Malik stared at her for one long, excruciating moment, then he reached toward her. His frame seemed to dwarf hers as she was pushed back farther in her seat. She kept her eyes on his. Even in the dimness of the car, she could see their piercing darkness absorbing her. Every muscle in her body tensed with expectation. When she heard a clicking sound she jumped, then settled as she realized he'd only unsnapped her seat belt.

The next couple of seconds were spent berating herself for thinking Malik was going to take her in his arms and kiss her senseless. She'd read scenes like this in books, the ones she didn't let anyone know she read. Her heart had pounded in her chest as the words formed some type of fantasy in her mind. She wanted to be swept away like a character in a romance novel, to be loved desperately by a man, her hero, and to live up to everything he wanted in a heroine.

From where she was sitting, she'd end up back in her apartment in bed with the ceiling fan on high and her pillows tucked between her legs to still the throbbing in about ten minutes. In her hand would be another one of those books, in her mind, her own fantasy. Reality was her life, the one she'd settled for and the one she was quickly beginning to hate.

In the middle of her thoughts his lips touched hers. She hadn't seen it coming because she'd been too deep in her own misery. But the splash of heat that hit her instantly as his lips brushed lightly over hers a second time was unmistakable.

"Relax," he whispered, his hand cupping her cheek, tilting her head upward to meet his next assault.

And it was exactly that, a slow brutal assault of each of her senses. His touch was soft, as if she was fragile and he didn't want to break her. When she inhaled— because otherwise she was sure to faint from the breath she wasn't aware she'd been holding—the scent of his cologne wafted through her like the freshness of a summer's rainfall. His voice had been a rough whisper that made her nipples go hard. Then his tongue stroked her bottom lip. She hurriedly traced her tongue along that same spot, loving the taste that slightly resembled the pizza they'd just eaten and the beer he'd consumed. That shouldn't have been sexy in the least bit, but it was. Oh, damn, damn, damn, it was.

Belinda kept her hands by her sides, didn't know what else to do with them. But that was okay because Malik knew precisely what to do with his. That one hand still cupped her cheek while the other moved to her shoulder, slipping behind her back so he could pull her closer. She had no idea that meant it would take the kiss deeper, but he did. And like a baby bird fresh out of the nest, she fell blindly into his embrace.

His mouth slanted over hers. She welcomed him, loving the feel of his tongue brushing along hers, swooshing deep inside her mouth then retreating to play a sensual little game with her lips. It seemed to last forever, but she knew logically it had only been a few seconds.

When he pulled back, it wasn't too far. If she nudged forward just an inch, she'd be kissing him again. But they both remained perfectly still.

"Is that the direction you want to go?" he asked, his voice even more gruff than it had been before, his eyes even darker.

Belinda swallowed and took a second to try and regain her senses. She wasn't sure what she wanted to say and that wasn't like her.

"I want more," was her final reply. "More out of life than what I've been getting."

"And you want that from me?"

When she didn't respond immediately, he pulled

back further, releasing his hold on her entirely. She felt cold instantly.

"I gave up games the minute that doctor told me I'd never play in the NBA again, Belinda. You need to be absolutely certain this is where you want to go because, once we take that step, there's no turning back."

He climbed out of the car before she could say another word. Which was probably better because again she didn't know what she wanted to say. If he were asking if she wanted his kisses, *hell yes* would be the immediate reply. But Belinda sensed Malik was asking much more of her than that. She'd never been impulsive, never did anything without considering all the consequences and repercussions—never really had to consider those things before. But Malik was right. They worked together, closely together. He was a part of her family even if not by blood. There was a lot at stake if they changed the boundaries of their relationship. She did need to be sure. She thought she was.

He stopped at her door, held out his hand for the key and let her inside.

"I'll see you at the bakery in the morning," he told her. Then after a moment he leaned forward and brushed his lips over her forehead. "Sleep tight," he whispered before walking away from her.

Belinda went into her apartment and did exactly as she'd predicted. Lying on her side with the pillow between her legs and her ceiling fan running on high, her bedroom windows opened a few inches, she tried to breathe through an internal heat that threatened to suffocate her. It wasn't that she simply wanted a man. She wanted Malik Anthony. That was a revelation that bore a lot of thinking. In which case she knew she wouldn't get any sleep tonight, even though Malik's last words to her sounded remarkably like her father's. Or probably because of that. She couldn't decide.

Chapter 5

"Either you're early or I'm extremely late," Carter Drayson said the moment Malik entered his office on Saturday morning.

It was nearing thirteen years that they'd known each other, and Malik figured Carter was the closest thing to a brother he was ever going to have. And he wasn't complaining. A more loyal and devoted friend he couldn't ask for—which only made Malik feel more like an ass for what he'd done last night. If there was one thing he knew about the Draysons, it was that they were a tight family. The men were very protective of the women and the women were all jewels in their own right. One particular jewel, the green-eyed one, held a special place in Lillian's and her parents' hearts. All of the above facts should have kept her wrapped in a neon DO NOT TOUCH sign.

But Malik had touched. And he'd tasted. And he'd

enjoyed. Much more than he'd enjoyed any other female he'd touched and tasted in his life. If he thought he'd wanted Belinda before, after last night he wasn't sure he'd be able to keep his hands off her again.

"I'm early. Wanted to talk to you for a sec before Drake arrived." Malik took a seat in one of the guest chairs across from Carter's desk.

"That actually works out because I wanted to talk to you, as well," Carter immediately replied.

And since Malik had a feeling what he wanted to say was of a more serious nature, he nodded and said, "It's your office, you go first."

"It's about a phone call I received. I'm trying to figure out how to handle it," Carter began.

"You make a date, take her out, then sleep with her. What, have you been doing this so long you're starting to doubt your abilities?" he asked with a chuckle.

"Ha. Ha," was Carter's glib reply. "This is serious, man. It's not about women."

To that Malik nodded. In Carter's mind the words *serious* and *women* were like oil and water and definitely did not mix. "Okay, tell me about this phone call."

"It was from Robinson Restaurants. You know the big conglomerate out of New York?"

Again Malik felt himself nodding and watching his friend carefully. "I've heard of them. Why are they calling you?"

"To offer me a job."

Now he raised a brow, sitting back in the chair and crossing one ankle on his opposite knee. "Really. Is that why you missed yesterday's meeting, because you were talking to the folks at Robinson?" Malik asked.

"No. Or yes. I guess you could say that. But good old

Dad filled me in on the meeting and I talked to Shari yesterday before she had to leave to pick up Andre." Carter sat back in his chair and looked away. "They want me to move to New York to be the executive pastry chef at their flagship restaurant."

Carter stared out of the one window in his office at the bakery. The other two walls were lined with bookshelves where he kept his portfolio—binder after binder filled with pictures of his renowned, lavishly decorated cakes. They sat on the oak wood shelves like trophies. Carter was proud of his work, he was confident and some would say he leaned heavily on the arrogant side. None of that bothered Malik because he knew the real Carter. He knew the young man who was struggling to prove his place in this family and who, because he considered himself his father's bastard love child, felt like an outsider.

That put them on common ground since Malik's father hadn't stuck around long enough for his birth, and his mother had struggled to raise him on her own, until she'd remarried a man old enough to be his grandfather. Then Malik had been whisked away from his inner-city home in south Philly, to a suburban neighborhood where he was the only African-American child walking around with a basketball cuffed under his arm.

They were both outsiders in their own way. And that realization prompted Malik's next words. "You're considering this offer, aren't you?"

"Why shouldn't I?" Carter asked. "It's a great offer. I'd finally be in charge of everything that went on in my kitchen. I could spread my wings and really show what I can do."

"And you don't do that here?"

"Are you serious? All of us work in the shadow of my grandmother. Not that I begrudge her any success. She's a wonderful woman and I've learned most of what I know from her. But I just feel like I'm trapped here. Like there's a place out there for me as Carter Drayson and not as Lillian Drayson's grandson."

"I hear you," Malik said. "But it's a big move. Your family will be disappointed."

"And that's the only reason I didn't tell Robinson yes right away. I know there's a lot more here than just a bakery. It's family and it's loyalty. I just have to figure out my place in it all."

"Whew." Malik let out a whoosh of breath. "That's heavy especially with the competition."

"I know they want to win. No news there."

"You don't sound excited," Malik noted.

Carter shrugged. "It's good exposure for the bakery," he replied. "I'll do my part."

"I'm sure you'll do more than your part. We're going to need you to pull out some fantastic designs for this one."

"I've thought of some new things, here and there." Carter looked up at Malik as if he'd just now realized he was sitting there and why. "But that's not what you want to talk to me about, is it?"

Malik rubbed a hand down the back of his head. "I guess it's all connected to what I wanted to say. I'm try-ing to figure out my place here, as well."

"What's that supposed to mean? You've been here for years and you're just as good a pastry chef as the rest of us."

Just as good, Malik thought with a sigh. He wondered if that would equate to him being good enough for Belinda.

"You know me well," Malik said with a sigh.

"Too well. So what's on your mind?"

"Belinda."

"What? Is she driving you crazy in the kitchen with her obsessive ways?" Carter laughed at his own questions. "Man, she's been like that all her life. You should have seen her the weekends I came to visit. She was even obsessive about playing games. You had to play precisely by her rules, no deviation. If we played dodge ball, she had to outline the boundaries for where the ball could go, where the person throwing the ball could stand. She was one uptight little girl. And now she's an uptight woman."

"With beautiful eyes and a kick-ass body," Malik added, knowing those words would effectively stop Carter's diatribe.

Carter did a double take then let a slow grin hover for a few seconds while he rubbed a hand over his chin.

"You looking at Belinda like that?"

Malik leaned forward, resting his elbows on his knees. "If I was, would that be a problem for you?"

"My first reaction is that might just be one of the stupidest decisions you've ever made," Carter replied.

Malik wasn't surprised. "She's a good woman," he countered because he'd never been the type of man to back down from something he decided he wanted.

"She's too much woman. I mean really, she's 'I'm Every Woman' that Chaka Khan and Whitney sang about. Everything has to be just right with her, all the time. She's even fanatical about her food touching on her plate. Is that something you want to deal with?"

The answer to Carter's question didn't readily come to Malik's mind because the lyrics to the song he'd mentioned were too busy playing like a broken record.

"I'm not intimidated by an accomplished woman. And you're her family, man. You shouldn't put her down like that."

Carter was shaking his head. "Not doing that at all," he told Malik. "I love my cousin and I know how hard she works and how good she is at what she does. But I also know she's got some issues that nobody in this family has ever wanted to deal with. She's intense, man. I figured she'd never get a man because she would always find something wrong with him."

"Maybe there was something wrong with the previous men she dated. Maybe they didn't know how to appreciate what they had."

"And you do? I mean, you think you can give Belinda what she needs?"

Malik paused. He took a deep breath then stood. "I don't know," he told Carter honestly.

"But you're willing to take that risk?"

"Life's about risks," Malik said, turning back to face Carter. "Each time I stepped out onto the floor to play ball I knew the risk of getting hurt. I did it anyway."

"And look where that landed you," Carter said.

Malik didn't take offense. The basis of his and Carter's friendship was brutal honesty. He could tell his friend when he was being an ass and could take it when Carter threw the same back at him. And he'd long since stopped feeling bad about tearing his ACL and being forced into retirement from the NBA.

"I never would have thought I'd become a pastry chef and actually enjoy it," he said with a slight chuckle. "My

life is so much fuller now than I think it would have
been if I'd continued playing ball. So what I'm saying
is that sometimes it's worth the risk."

Carter nodded. "You sound like you've been giving
this a lot of thought."

"I've been thinking about your cousin for longer than
I care to admit. Now I think it might be our time."

"You've got that right," Drake said, walking into
the office with his briefcase and a smile that said business was good.

"Gentlemen, I come to you today with a proposition
that's going to make us, meaning the male portion of
the dynamic baking talent at Lillian's, look like movie
stars. It is definitely *our* time."

Carter and Malik shared a quizzical glance while
Drake closed the door.

"Sit down, Malik. We're going to need some of your
connections for this, too."

Malik wasn't sure what Drake meant by that but went
along with him and took a seat.

"So the blog's been doing phenomenal. I mean we're
getting close to twenty thousand hits per day. But it's
that little impromptu baking lesson we did and put on
YouTube that landed this newest offer on our doorstep."

Drake was excited. Then again, he was always excited when he talked about promoting the bakery.

For the past two months Carter, Drake and Malik
had been hosting a blog called *Brothers Who Bake*. Of
course, it had been Drake's idea and Carter had immediately agreed, which meant Malik was outnumbered.
Good thing for him he'd thought it was a good idea to
promote the bakery and to possibly get more men to
enter the kitchen or more women to leave the kitchen

to come into the bakery and place an order. Their statistics showed they were doing pretty decent in both areas.

"Wait a minute. I thought we were only doing the YouTube thing once," Carter said to Drake when they were all seated.

"Yeah, but it's getting some really good feedback. So good, this guy James Bandenski contacted me."

"Who's James Bandenski?" Malik asked.

"He's an editor at Cresston Press. They publish a lot of nonfiction books, some textbooks and a good number of cookbooks."

When neither Malik nor Carter said anything to that, Drake sighed. Malik and Carter shared a glance and a chuckle. They loved to annoy Drake. He was such an easy target and it reminded them of their college days when their frat brothers fell victim to their pranks. Actually, this was the highly matured version of the young men they'd been back then. There's no telling what they would have done to Drake ten years ago.

"And he wants the Brothers Who Bake to write a cookbook," Drake said, excitement all but dripping from his already jovial personality.

"A cookbook," Carter repeated, looking less than excited about the idea.

"I'm a baker—" Malik replied and was stopped mid-sentence.

Drake held up a hand. "Don't even say it. I know you're a baker, not a writer. Ha. Ha."

Malik chuckled and Carter joined in, knowing instinctively that Malik was referring to the famous Michael Jackson quote "I'm a lover, not a fighter." Apparently, after all these years working together, Drake was just as tuned in to him as Carter was.

"Can we be serious for a minute? This would be major for us. Coupled with winning the cake competition, we'll be set. Next year we could start looking at expanding outside Chicago. This could be it!" Drake said excitedly.

Carter nodded. "And since it's your idea, it could also buy you some brownie points with Grandma and maybe she'll leave the bakery to you."

An instant chill filled the air. Malik had been around this family for long enough to know about the camaraderie between the grandchildren. It was no secret that Lillian would be leaving control of the bakery to one of them someday soon. Lately that day seemed a lot closer. Each of them thought they could run the bakery, and probably could, but Lillian would only name one. Was Drake vying for this position?

"This benefits us all," Drake replied. "Don't you agree, Malik?"

Always the tiebreaker, Malik took a second to consider Drake's proposal.

"Like anything in business it's good to strike while the iron's hot. We've built up momentum with the blog, then the YouTube video took us up another notch. I took your suggestion from the notes you gave me the other day and started tweeting about the blog. I heard from a few of my old NBA buddies as a result so there's a definite buzz going. With that said, it's obvious doing this cookbook will only push us further into the spotlight, just like the competition," he said.

"That's what I'm saying," Drake hurriedly chimed in.

"But," Malik added, "it's a tremendous responsibility on all of our parts. And speaking for myself I'd have to say, I'm pretty busy as it is. I mean, what we'd have to consider is if this is something we all want to dedicate time to."

"I don't know," Carter said instantly.

"You don't know about becoming famous for your work?" Drake asked with a questioning glare.

Carter shook his head. "I'm already well-known for my work, Drake. Besides, this is totally different. You're asking us to sit down and write recipes. The recipes we use here are mostly Grandma's. We can't really put them in a book and slap the name Brothers Who Bake onto it. That's misrepresentation."

Drake looked a little deflated but he nodded in agreement. "I didn't say what the outline of the book had to be. We could come up with that on our own. Malik," he said, turning in his chair to stare at Malik. "What if you used the recipe for those cookies you came up with last fall, the ones with the Belgian chocolate chunks and maple syrup? And those mint brownies. Those are your recipes. Carter, you could have a section on cake design. Take them through the basics and only up to the point where they might be competition for you. I have some new filling flavors I've been toying with. We can do this," he said emphatically.

Malik thought about what he'd said and had to admit he thought it was a possibility. He just didn't want to totally commit right now, not with this competition coming up and with things between him and Belinda in limbo.

"Why don't we all think about it a little more? Is there a deadline for when we need to get back to the editor?" Malik asked.

"No," Drake said. "Nothing etched in stone but I'm sure he's not going to wait forever."

"We're not going to take forever," Carter interjected. "Calm down, man. Let's just sleep on this a night or so then meet up again to see where we are, like Malik said."

Drake nodded. "Okay, but a few days and then we meet."

"You said no deadline," Malik told Drake as he stood.

"I said the editor didn't have a deadline. I'm giving you two one of my own. Because you," he said, pointing to Carter, "I know how you are between your personal exploits and work. I'm not giving you time to forget."

"What about me?" Malik asked jokingly.

It was Drake's turn to chuckle. "You don't have a personal life. When's the last time you went out on a date?"

Carter laughed, as well.

So now the joke was on him?

"As a matter of fact, I was out last night with a gorgeous female," he said, giving Carter a pointed look.

He left the office to questions like, "Who was she?" and "Did you pay her to go out with you?" Both questions came from Drake, who had no idea Malik had been referring to his sister. Carter didn't say a word, because he knew.

Malik left with a smile and an extra pep in his step. He was going to pursue Belinda Drayson-Jones, finally.

Daisy Drayson-Jones was still a very attractive woman at fifty-two. She was tall, five-nine, having inherited her height from her father, and her figure had only mildly filled out over the years and after the birth of two children, Belinda and Drake. Matt always joked how he loved some cushioning in his women, as if they hadn't been married for thirty years, and he probably couldn't remember the last woman he was with before her. It was all right, though, because Matt was her soul mate. She'd known that the day she had met him as she'd walked along the college campus. The years that followed were full of happy times getting to know her husband then having their children.

These days, with her children grown and Matt taken to his newest hobby—which he swore was going to morph into a phenomenal career—golfing, Daisy utilized her accounting/business management degree to take care of the executive decisions dealing with the bakery. Her mother had gradually been asking her to do more, something that used to be a heated debate between the two. As Lillian's sole daughter, it seemed only right that Daisy take over the helm at the bakery. But baking, while she was good at it, had never really called to Daisy. Working behind the scenes on the business aspect was more her speed. So for the years she was home raising her children, she was also the part-time accountant and business manager for the bakery, a job which undoubtedly rubbed off on her son.

Today, however, Daisy wasn't thinking about business. She was thinking about her daughter, who had everything a young successful woman could ever want. Everything except happiness.

Belinda made her way toward the terrace seat at McCormick & Schmick's, her long legs showing beneath the just-above-the-knee Krista silk bubble dress she'd given her for her birthday. It was a pretty royal blue print that perfectly accented Belinda's light coloring. With a burst of pride, Daisy smiled as a couple of men did double takes when Belinda walked past.

"Hi, Mama," Belinda said, leaning forward to kiss her mother's cheek before taking her seat.

The child had been oblivious to the men staring at her. At times Daisy grew concerned at just how many things Belinda didn't pay attention to. Like the fact that her biological clock would be ticking sooner rather than later if she didn't hurry up and find herself a husband.

"Hi, baby," she replied. "You look pretty today."

"Thanks." Belinda gave her mother a small smile. She pulled the napkin off the table and placed it in her lap before she looked up at Daisy again. "You look nice, too. Did Franco do something different to your hair?"

Daisy ran her fingers quickly through the short silky strands of her bronze frosted hair. "Yes. It's a new color and a cut. He called it sassy." She shook her head again for effect. "I like it."

Belinda chuckled. "I like it, too. But what did Daddy have to say? You know he likes you with longer hair."

Daisy waved a hand. "Your father can't see past that golf ball and those putt sticks."

"Golf clubs, Mama. You know that's what they're called."

"I know what I'd like to call them," Daisy replied instead. "But I don't want to talk about him. Let's hurry up and order so I can get to what I really want to say."

As much as she tried to delay, Belinda knew the moment had finally come.

"So you know the cocktail party is coming up next weekend," Daisy said as she sipped the coffee she'd ordered after finishing her salmon over pasta.

"What cocktail party?" Belinda asked, hoping if she acted clueless her mother would skip this subject entirely.

With a cock of her head and a knowing look Daisy killed that dream.

"The NAACP fund-raiser I host every year. Come, Belinda, ignorance is not attractive."

And neither was what was about to come next.

"Right. Where are you having it this year?"

"At the Ivy Room. That place Sylvia selected last year was just not the answer. So anyway, I was wondering if you've purchased your dress."

That was so not what her mother was wondering. But Belinda was determined not to give an inch today.

"No. Not yet."

Daisy folded her napkin over once, and another time for good measure, then looked at Belinda with one eyebrow raised. "And a date?"

"Do I really need a date to attend a fund-raiser? It's just a cocktail party."

"It's a big event that puts the family name right up there with some of the most influential people in this city. Your grandparents aren't attending this year and neither are my brothers. Someone has to represent us."

"I thought Drake said he was going."

"That's right, and so are you."

Belinda nodded. Of course she was because she did everything she was told.

"I'll find a dress this week," she said, feeling a little deflated at giving in when she'd said she wouldn't. At least her mother hadn't offered to set her up with a date. That was something.

"Helga Livingston's son Hugo is in town."

Belinda groaned. She couldn't help it. And Daisy frowned.

"That's rude, Belinda."

"Sorry. But really, I don't need a date."

"You most certainly do. You are an eligible young lady. And to tell you the truth, your father and I would like grandchildren before we're confined to a home."

"Really, Mom? You're in your early fifties. I don't see you or Daddy in a home anytime soon. Besides, Drake is perfectly capable of finding a wife and having some kids."

"Men tend to take their time," Daisy said with another wave of her hand. "But I expect more from my daughter."

Of course she did. They all expected more from her. "I'm perfectly capable of getting my own date. As a matter of fact, I've managed to beat you to the punch this time."

That perked Daisy up. "You did? Who is he? Do I know his parents?"

"No. I don't think you do," was Belinda's immediate response.

"Well, who is he?" she was still asking as Belinda pulled out her wallet and slipped her credit card into the case with the check.

"He's only coming as my date for the evening, Mama. It's not an audition for husband and father of the year," Belinda told her.

Daisy shook her head. "I'm just curious."

"Curiosity killed the cat," Belinda snapped, then looked at her mother with a wan smile. "I'll be at the cocktail party and I'll have a date. All will be well."

But later Belinda wondered just how she was going to come through with that promise, since she had neither a dress nor a date for next Saturday night.

Chapter 6

"What are you doing still here?" Belinda asked the minute she entered the kitchen at the bakery to the sweet smell of brownies baking.

"I think it's self-explanatory," Malik said, looking up only momentarily from the walnuts he was meticulously chopping, and offering her a smile.

It hit her right in the gut, that smile of his that showed perfect white teeth and a deep dimple she hadn't noticed before in his left cheek. His eyebrows were thick, not bushy but thick and dark like his hair, his chin strong, his jaw chiseled. Desire trickled slowly down her spine, like water dripping from a faucet, gaining momentum each time she was close to Malik.

She'd reprimanded herself about her thoughts where he was concerned more than a few times since their date last night. It was foolish to believe that a night of wild, uninhibited sex would make a life-altering difference in her world. And maybe, at this stage of the game, it was kind of silly to think Malik would even want a night of wild, uninhibited sex with her. Yet he'd been just as into that kiss last night as she was. And he'd told her, to be sure. Watching the fit of his jeans over taut buttocks as he went to the oven and removed a tray of beautiful, perfect Blondies, she was sure of one thing—Malik Anthony was one fine male specimen.

Belinda cleared her throat, putting down her purse on the table by the door and moving closer to where he had boxes already filled with cookies. Malik made the best cookies. His peanut butter cups and Turtles were her favorites.

"We're closed on Sundays, remember? What are you making all this for?"

"Spring tournament tomorrow down at the rec center. I bring all the desserts," he told her.

"What kind of tournament? Basketball?" She presumed it was basketball because of his past but immediately thought she could just as well be wrong.

He nodded, setting the tray of brownies on the table and taking a peek into another oven that held more. There were timers all over the kitchen but nobody used them unless they were in a rush and had lots of orders to fill. Other than that they all sort of knew when their stuff was done.

"The nonprofit youth program I head up has an annual basketball tournament every April. It's also our only fund-raiser for the summer camp each year."

Malik talked while he worked, explaining this as simply as if he were telling her the ingredients of his Turtle cookies, which she'd already asked him for and he would not divulge.

"So you work with the youth?" Why did that surprise her?

He spared her a glance and shook his head. "There's a lot you don't know about me, Belinda. Yes, I work with the youth. I started Hoop'n Stars after I left the NBA, because I wanted to keep active and I also wanted to give inner-city youth some of the opportunities I never had."

Wow, she thought in her mind but wisely did not say. "You're right, I guess there's a lot I don't know about you."

"Do you want to know more about me?" he asked her.

"We work together, spend a lot of time together, I guess it makes sense that I know who I'm elbow to elbow with on some days," she replied lightly.

"Come on, you can do better than that. Give me a straight answer. Would you like to get to know me better?"

He stood up straight, grabbed a bowl of icing for his sugar and spice cookies that he topped with sweet buttercream in an array of bright colors.

He looked at her seriously, expectantly. It made her a little nervous, but she'd be damned if she showed him that. Squaring her shoulders and folding her arms over her chest, she replied, "Yes, I would."

Malik nodded, then returned his attention to the cookies. For what seemed like forever she watched him work, his large hands maneuvering the spatula with ease, leaving a light and airy twist to the icing on each cookie. He'd done a complete sheet in a pretty pink shade before she finally spoke up.

"So you'll play ball all day and then the teams will

fill up on brownies and cookies?" She tried to make the question seem light and not too probing even though she found herself extremely interested in this program he'd instituted.

"Different teams from around the city will play each other until there's only one left standing. Even cheerleaders attend and hold their own competition. There'll be lots of vendors from around the city, all of whom do something relating to children. That's the focus— the youth, because they're our future. There's a local deli that donates sandwiches and chips and hot dogs. Some of the parents—the ones who are active in their children's lives—also bring dishes. But I always bring the desserts. It's a fun and eventful day. You should join me."

"Me? I don't know what I'd do at an event like this." Sort of like she never had any idea what to do at the NAACP fund-raiser her mother produced every year, yet she went anyway.

"You could sit on the bench and cheer when my team wins," he said with a teasing grin that had her wrapping her arms even tighter around her chest. Her breasts were having one wicked reaction to this man and his smiles.

"Or you could help serve the desserts." He came back with a follow-up.

"What time is it and where?"

He looked up so fast Belinda thought he would drop the spatula. "You serious?"

She nodded. "Sure. I'm not doing anything else tomorrow. And you've baked enough to feed a small army," she said, looking around the kitchen. "I'm sure it'll be hard for you to coach a team and distribute the desserts."

"Some of the parents usually help. But I'd love to have you there."

His words seemed so sincere and Belinda was just hungry enough for true sincerity she lapped them up quickly with her own smile. "Then it's a date," she said happily. "I mean, I'll be there."

"It's a date," he corrected her, and stared at her so long she almost ran across the room, jumped on him and kissed him.

That would have taken them both by surprise. So much so she had to laugh it off as she turned away from him and took a deep, steadying breath.

On the opposite table from where Malik worked, there were five boxes, white with the pink swirling logo of Lillian's. They each held two dozen cookies. Belinda walked the length of the table, peeking inside each box. She stopped in front of the one at the end.

"Go ahead and take one. You know you want to," she heard him say.

Belinda looked over her shoulder. "I didn't say I wanted one of your cookies."

Malik chuckled and came over to stand beside her. "You don't have to. I know you love the Turtles."

Of course he was right but she didn't want to admit it, so she didn't reach for a cookie. It didn't seem to matter, because in the next moment Malik was taking a cookie out of the box and stepping closer to her.

"I know what you want, Belinda," he said, bringing the cookie to her lips.

He was close enough to touch, close enough that her nipples had instantly grown hard. He said he knew what she wanted, but she was afraid Malik had absolutely no idea.

She opened her mouth to accept the cookie, took a bite of the soft, gooey sweetness and moaned as she chewed. She couldn't help herself. "I don't know what you put in these cookies but I swear I've never tasted anything like this before." She talked as she finished chewing then licked her lips.

When she looked up at him again it was to see that his eyes had grown darker, his face a little more intense than it had looked just seconds ago.

"They're really good," she said, standing a little straighter.

Malik took the remaining half of the cookie into his mouth and chewed, then licked his lips just as she had. Something swirled in the pit of her stomach, settling in a heated ball right between her legs.

"Thank you," he said, his voice a timbre lower than it had been before. He moved a little closer. "You missed a bit of caramel."

Her fingers immediately went to her lips. "Where?"

He grabbed her wrist, pulling away her hand from her mouth. "Here," he said, dipping his head lower to lick the caramel from the corner of her mouth. "And here." He licked the other corner.

She wanted to close her legs, tight. No, she wanted her pillow. It had offered her plenty of comfort in the previous nights.

"I think you missed a spot, too," she heard herself whispering, and traced her tongue over his bottom lip.

She was overwhelmed with boldness. First, volunteering to spend the day with him, then licking his lips like she'd been forever his lover. This was not the norm for her and yet it felt good, wildly, excitingly good.

On the last stroke of her tongue over his lip, Malik's

arms came roughly around her waist, pulling her until her body was flush against his. Belinda went willingly, loving the sting of dominance and the exhilaration of arousal that swept over her. His mouth took hers then in a fevered rush of dueling tongues and muted moans. Her arms went around his neck, pulling him closer, her hands flattening on his shoulders, fingers clenching, gripping. She wanted something she couldn't explain, something she'd never wanted before, and Malik seemed like he was game to give it to her.

He walked her backward until she was against one of the Sub-Zero refrigerators. Momentarily he pulled his lips from hers. "You're driving me crazy," he murmured. "You've always driven me crazy." Then there were no more words, just his mouth blazing a scorching path from her lips, over her cheek, down her neck.

His strong hands had gripped her bottom, squeezing each side until her knees threatened to give out. Then he ran his hands along her thighs and Belinda didn't know what else to do but lift one of her legs. Malik groaned, pulling her leg and wrapping it around his waist. He thrust forward, his erection rubbing flush against her heated center. She sighed, bit her bottom lip to hold back a scream and let her head fall back until it rapped against the refrigerator door.

Malik kept going, his mouth touching every inch of her bared skin he could find. When there was no more skin, he settled for the material-covered mound of her breasts and nibbled there. *Wanting her* was an understatement. He was actually so hard that he'd surpassed the *need* phase and was coming up on sheer desperation. He moved his hand from her leg, tracing the inside of her thigh until he cupped her center. She hissed and made some other sound that was close to a purr and by far the sexiest thing he'd ever heard.

Bing!

The timer sounded and both of them froze. It took about three seconds for Belinda to flatten her hands on his chest and start to push him away. And another five seconds for his lust-riddled brain to figure out what was going on and ease away from her slowly.

Her usually neat-as-a-pin hair was ruffled, her eyes darker, like the raging sea. She was breathing as heavily as he was, her lips swollen from his rough kisses, the skin along her neck slightly bruised from his suckling and licking. In short, looking at her now made him feel like an ass. A very needy ass, but still.

"I apologize," he said immediately. "That was way out of line."

She'd begun to shake her head, then closed her eyes. As she took a deep breath Malik damned himself to hell by staring at the rise and fall of her full breasts, the curve of her hips and the juncture between her legs he'd just touched.

"Your brownies," she said finally.

He'd had to tear away his gaze from her body to look her in the eye. "What?"

She pointed to the oven. "Your brownies are going to burn. The time is up."

He cursed under his breath, turning away from her and finding an oven mitt so he could pull out the two trays. Placing each tray on the table, he sighed heavily.

"They don't look like they burned," Belinda said as she looked them over.

Malik shook his head. "They'll be too dry. The Belgian chocolate center should ooze when you bite into it. Cooking it past twenty-five minutes cooks it to a cakelike consistency."

"Sorry. I shouldn't have interrupted you."

Malik had to smile. "I'll take your interruption over brownies any day."

He was rewarded with her smile in return. "I'll just have to start over."

"I can help," she volunteered and again her words were like music to his ears. He hadn't wanted her to leave, even though he still had a lot of baking to do. And now she'd offered to stay so he wouldn't seem like the desperate sap he was sure he was becoming over this woman.

"That'd be great," he replied and watched as she moved to the cabinets near the door and retrieved her apron.

Betty Boop was looking even sexier now that he'd gotten his hands on the body beneath.

The Charleston Baynor-Hill Recreation Center in Englewood wasn't a building Belinda was familiar with. And while she'd lived in Chicago all her life, she'd never been to this south Chicago neighborhood. Not until this morning when she'd come in behind Malik, carrying all the cookies and brownies they'd stayed at the bakery until well after midnight baking. The main foyer was decorated with flyers about all their upcoming events and pictures of the basketball team, swim team, cheer-leaders, youth leaders and more, all smiling happily. It was a contrast to what Malik had told her to expect.

"These kids didn't grow up like you did, Belinda. They've never been on an estate like the one you lived in with Lillian and your parents. Hell, they'll probably never see an estate in their lifetime. Life's been pretty rough for them, and in most cases still is. I just don't want you experiencing a culture shock."

She'd taken offense to that remark and replied with, "I'm not some diva on her high horse, Malik. I know that I was blessed to have the upbringing I did and I don't look down on anyone who didn't."

He'd apologized profusely and Belinda had decided to let it go. The old Belinda would have cursed him all around Hyde Park and back, then got out of the truck and went home. She figured that's probably why he'd made the comment in the first place. Malik knew all about the old Belinda. He just didn't know how she'd committed to making changes in her life.

After she'd been there for about an hour, Belinda found herself enjoying the event. They were still in the setup stage, but already a few of the kids were arriving.

"Each coach needs to sign in their team when they get here. That goes for the cheerleaders, too," Malik was telling a tall woman with ebony hair cascading silkily down her back. She looked like she could be of African-American and Asian mixture, then again, those eyes could be a great job done with eyeliner.

"I'll take care of it, Malik. You know I know how this works. This is my third year working with you," she'd said, her long—too long to be real—lashes fluttering wildly.

Belinda tried hard not to be judgmental. Really, she did. But she had a good idea what was on this woman's agenda and it didn't have a damn thing to do with these kids.

"Okay, fine. I'll just be over here getting the food organized."

"Oh, I can help with that, too, since the coaches aren't here," Lash Lady said with a smile.

"That's okay. I already have help in that department," Malik told her and cast a glance over to the booth where Belinda was standing, staring at them like they were the next best thing to a daily soap opera.

He'd already begun walking away from her and was coming around to her side of the booth when he said, "That's Mrs. Martin. Her son Jarrod is my star forward. He's thirteen and plays like he might have a future. I've arranged for a couple of great high school coaches to come today and have a look at him. Otherwise, I might be tempted to ask her to leave."

"I could ask her to leave if you'd like," Belinda replied, only half playing. The woman was still looking over at their booth, but this time at her and not Malik. She was giving Belinda the stink-eye and was planning how she could mark her territory—meaning Malik. Belinda almost laughed.

"No. I'll need her permission to have the high school coaches talk to Jarrod so I don't want to piss her off."

She nodded. "I see."

Malik laughed from behind her. "You know when I'm talking quietly to you about somebody it sort of gives me away if you're staring them in the face."

Belinda shrugged and begrudgingly turned away. "She's got a pretty face."

"Pretty is the face you look at in the mirror every day," he said, not even bothering to look at her. For the third time since they'd left the bakery he was counting the boxes they'd yet to unpack.

"Thanks, but pretty's not all it's cracked up to be,"

was her tight reply. "And I believe we have more than enough desserts."

"You never know," he said, finally turning to her.

He stepped closer and, with a finger, tilted her chin so she was looking up at him.

"Pretty is just fine with me."

"I'm sure," she said with a nod toward Mrs. Martin.

"What? Please, that woman's crazy with a capital *C* and I try my best to stay away from Capital *C* people."

She didn't reply.

"Jealous?" he asked with a raise of an eyebrow.

No. Or at least she didn't plan on being very long. Placing her hands on his chest Belinda pushed him away. "You wish," she said playfully even though she could still feel Mrs. Martin's heated gaze on her.

About an hour later the cheerleading competition kicked off with the youngest groups competing first. From the dessert stand Belinda could see the majority of the girls as they huddled with their team then stepped out onto the mats to perform. She watched with just a tinge of envy inside.

Her mother was adamant that cheerleading was not something Belinda would ever do. There were no social or economic benefits to the sport, her mother had said. When she was young, Belinda hadn't cared about a benefit. She'd just wanted to join the other girls her age, hoping in this one event they would let her in, let her be a part of their group instead of always ostracizing her because she was smarter and, as her mother said, prettier than them. She'd just wanted to belong. But that never happened. Daisy was adamant and her grandmother came up with the idea of Belinda spending her free time at the bakery with her instead. So much for her having a say in her personal life then and even now.

As the teams competed, Belinda watched the mothers on the sidelines. Wearing shirts in matching team colors, they cheered on their girls. How wonderful it must feel to have that type of support, Belinda thought, to know that your mother was just as excited by this sport as you were. One little girl stood out. Or rather she sat out, on the end of the bottom bleacher all alone.

Belinda watched her for a few minutes just to be sure she was by herself. She didn't know why it mattered or what she could even do to help, but before she could stop herself Belinda was headed toward the bleachers. The second competition for an older group was just getting under way when she sat on the bleacher beside the girl.

"Wow, how do they do that?" she asked by way of breaking the ice.

"It takes a lot of practice. I practice all the time," the girl said.

"I bet you're really good."

She shrugged. Her hair was pulled back into a messy ponytail and there were silver stud earrings in her ears. Belinda had noticed the other girls had sparkly stuff in their hair, headbands and scrunchies. This little girl didn't.

"You practice every day after school?" Belinda asked.

She nodded again. "And on the weekends. Whenever I come here to the rec, I can practice flips and stuff. I do that a lot, too."

Which meant she spent a lot of time away from home.

"I'll bet your mother's really proud."

Another shrug of the shoulders. "She works a lot, so she doesn't really know what I'm doing."

"Oh," Belinda said as if she understood. But she didn't, not at all.

Each day when Belinda came home from school, her mother had been there. Her father would be at work and she'd see him later that evening at dinner. And when they'd lived on the estate with her grandparents, her grandfather was always there to greet her. After homework she'd play with Shari and Drake and Carter if he was there. Monica was younger so they didn't play with her as often. But the point was there was never a time Belinda could actually say she was alone, or alone enough to make a decision on her own about how she'd spend her time.

"What's your name?" she asked, suddenly wanting to know more about this little girl and her life.

"Kayla Washington," was her reply. "Are you a recruiter?" she asked, her eyes perking up a little more.

"No," Belinda responded with her own measure of disappointment. Clearly this little girl was looking for a way out of her situation, whatever that situation was. "But I'd love to see you perform," she told her.

"Sure, I guess that's okay. My team's up next," Kayla said and stood.

She took off the denim jacket she'd been wearing and Belinda could see her uniform hung a little loose on Kayla. It appeared the girl wasn't eating as well as she should, either. As Kayla moved to the mat, Belinda made a mental note to talk to her coach sometime before the day was over. If there was anything she could do for Kayla, she wanted to do it. Not only because of the girl's need but because there was something Kayla had given her today—a glimpse of the girlhood she could have had. And a deeper glimpse of the pure optimism of a child. Kayla believed a recruiter would come along, see how good she was and give her a scholarship, a way out of her old life and into a new one.

If Kayla could believe that, Belinda could, too. If she stood up and reached for what she wanted, the same way Kayla was now, climbing to the top of that pyramid and reaching both arms out into the air, she could be happy. Just like the big smile that covered Kayla's face. Belinda could be really happy.

Six hours into the day and Belinda was still going strong, Malik noted. She smiled and joked with a lot of the parents—minus Mrs. Martin—and she played with the kids. When she wasn't passing out cookies, she was watching the cheerleading competition, cheering for one particular girl. When that girl—Malik thought her name was Kayla from the middle school in the neighborhood—had advanced with her team another round, Belinda had clapped and screamed like one of the parents.

The minute the girl ran off the mats, she went straight to Belinda, who'd welcomed her with a big hug. He wondered if she'd known the girl before and made it a point to ask her the minute she returned to the booth.

"She was the only one on the team without her mother cheering her on. She works two jobs..." Belinda told him. "I didn't want her to feel like nobody cared how well she was doing."

He simply stared at her for a moment.

"What?" she demanded.

"Nothing," Malik said, shaking his head. "You just keep shocking me."

"I could say the same about you, Coach Anthony."

She touched his arm before leaving him to pass out more cookies. That touch sent heat soaring through his body. It was no secret to Malik that he wanted this woman on a physical level. But she was right, there was a lot he didn't know about her. Sure, he knew her family and what she did for a living, and he knew she was unhappy. But there were other things about Belinda Drayson-Jones that were pleasantly surprising him. One was that she apparently really liked children. Another was how deeply his need for her had obviously grown over the years, until now he could only pray she was on the same page.

Chapter 7

She should invite him into her apartment and kiss him. Their kisses always led to heated passion, so the next step would be inevitable. She would seduce him. That was Belinda's final decision as she rode in the passenger seat of the bakery truck Malik had used to transport them and all the goodies they'd provided at the tournament.

He parked in the garage and came up to her apartment with her, just as she'd suspected. Giving him her key, she waited while he unlocked the door for her, just as he did the night after their date. This time as she stepped inside she said, "You want to come in for a while?"

The air around them held a distinct sizzle as Malik waited a beat to respond.

"Sure," he said almost hesitantly.

Or that might have been her imagination since her

heart was beating so fast and loud she could barely hear her own thoughts, let alone perceive anything he hadn't actually said.

Malik had been to her apartment before so he was relaxed enough to walk into the living room and take a seat. Belinda on the other hand was taking deep breaths with every step she took. Normally, to her, the apartment looked fine. Everything in its place, right down to the three magazines neatly stacked on the glass coffee table—because four or more was too much. This was her living room not a waiting room for the public. Her couch and love seat were a deep caramel color with pretty sage-colored paisley pillows that were precisely puffed and arranged in each corner. There was a steel and cherrywood sofa table and mirror to the right of the closet, just inside the doorway. She always laid her purse there.

Tonight, though, she was so nervous she went into the dining room and turned on the CD player because she thought music would be good, before she realized she hadn't put her purse down. With a silent curse she walked back, passing Malik as he sat on the couch, to lay her purse neatly on the left corner of the sofa table. A quick glance in the mirror showed her just how nervous she was. Her eyes looked as if they might actually pop out of her head. For a second she just stood still, trying to steady her breathing.

When she thought she could actually speak without making a fool of herself, Belinda returned to the living room and asked, "Would you like something to drink? Beer or wine?"

Malik cocked his head and simply stared at her. Today he'd worn another pair of jeans—denim was made for this man, she was absolutely sure of it. The fit was perfect over his muscled thighs and firm buttocks. Too many times today she'd stopped herself from touching him, just once. But the urge was still there. And his arms, when had his biceps begun to look as delectable as her favorite dessert? It was as insane as the instant heat she felt when she was near him.

And here's the conclusion she'd finally come to—she was very attracted to Malik Anthony. Not that she'd never noticed before how handsome he was, but in these past couple days, there had been a little more to him and whatever that was pulled at her like a magnet.

"You don't have any beer in that refrigerator," he said in a mocking tone. She was sure of the tone as she'd been staring at his lips as he talked, and heard him clearly.

"How do you know?" she asked, trying not to immediately grow defensive.

He grinned. A sexy-ass grin that made her want to run across that room and straddle him.

His response was to get up and walk toward the kitchen. Of course that meant he had to pass her. She gulped in anticipation of his proximity and almost screamed when his bare arm brushed against hers as he moved by. The contact was like electricity, buzzing wild between the two of them. With every bit of strength she could muster, Belinda tried to remain calm. She took deep breaths and used one hand to fan herself quickly while his back was still turned to her.

"See," he yelled from the kitchen, "cran-grape juice, water bottles and a two liter of diet ginger ale. Just as I suspected."

By this time Belinda had walked into the kitchen,

one hand on her hip as she stood directly behind Malik, who had one hand on the door of the refrigerator, holding it wide-open.

"What? Do you memorize what I have in my house?" she asked, trying to push the door closed.

It was futile since he was much taller and significantly stronger than her. Not that he was exuding any of his strength; he just stood his ground while she pushed around him in a useless and probably totally ridiculous fashion. That thought caused her to stop. Instead she stepped to the side.

"Close the door or pay my utility bill." She'd tried to sound irritated, or at the very least in control of her emotions. But it didn't sound very convincing, even to her.

Malik's response—which should have been anticipated and expected—was to laugh.

"You always drink the same thing. Beer and alcohol are not on the list."

"I drink wine," she said haughtily.

"Your preference is white and you only drink at dinner."

She blinked for a moment because how the hell could he manage to still look good while insulting her?

"I'm not predictable," was her reply.

He closed the refrigerator door then. "No," he said seriously, "you're not. I'm beginning to figure that out about you and it's sort of a surprise."

"Why? Because everybody thinks they know me so well?"

He nodded. "I guess you could say that."

They stood face-to-face now. She was fed up, riled up, turned on and generally about to crack up if she didn't do something fast. It was now or never, she thought.

Take what you want. Do what you want. Go for it!

The words played over and over in her head until she found herself taking a step forward.

"You have no idea who I really am or what I want," she told him. "Maybe it's time I show you."

To his credit Malik didn't move an inch. He simply stood there like the honey-toned, too-fine-for-his-own-good man that he was. Her courage only faltered a millisecond as she stepped even closer to him. It was like an invisible cloak had instantly wrapped itself around her so that she felt safe and protected. Feelings she'd previously accredited to her self-defense classes and the Mace she carried in her purse at all times. Never, in all her twenty-six years, had she attributed them to a man.

Belinda was five foot seven, and on most days she wore four- to five-inch heels. And she didn't consider herself skinny with all the curves she'd had since she'd turned fifteen. So feeling small and feminine around men wasn't usually something she experienced. Until now.

"Make sure you know what you're doing, Belinda," was his tight reply.

She barely paid attention to his words. She was so intent on touching him, finally. His biceps were where she placed her hands, rubbing her fingers lightly along the taut skin over muscle and sighing inwardly.

"I'm sure you've heard how smart I am, graduated summa cum laude from Yale," she told him, watching her hand move over his muscles.

When her hands moved from his biceps to flatten over his toned pecs, it was Malik who sucked in a breath. The action startled Belinda and she looked up into his eyes. He was staring down at her hands on his chest, his lips drawn in a tight line, a muscle ticking on the right side of his jaw. Acting purely on instinct, she glided her hands over his pecs once more, letting her fingertips run slowly over his nipples.

Malik took in a deep breath, lifted his hands to wrap his fingers slowly around her wrists.

"I'm only going to warn you once more, Belinda. Know exactly what you're doing. Because I don't know how much longer I can hold back with you."

She was shaking her head before he could finish speaking, before he could look at her, his eyes dark with what she thought was desire.

"I know exactly what I'm doing. And I don't want you to hold back," she told him. It was the most honest thing she'd ever said in her life. The truest statement to ever leave her lips.

For endless moments their gazes locked, her hands on him, his on her. They were perfectly still in her kitchen.

In the next instant Malik had wrapped her arms around his neck and slid his hands down her arms, to her bottom, which he grabbed and squeezed with so much pressure Belinda almost swooned. Before she could take a breath, he was lifting her into the air, wrapping her legs around his waist the way he'd done her arms around his neck.

He was walking her to the bedroom when his lips touched hers softly. "You won't regret this," he whispered over her lips but Belinda's body was so on fire for him she didn't have time to examine his words.

Inside her bedroom he set her slowly onto her bed.

He went to the bedside tables and turned on the lamps. Light flooded the room, slicing through the veil of desire she'd been draped in.

"Both lights?" she asked.

Malik came to stand in front of her so she had to crane her neck to see him.

"I've waited so long to see you. There's no way in hell I'm going to miss a single inch of that gorgeous body."

In the grand scheme of things this wasn't the most romantic thing Belinda imagined hearing. But she wouldn't think about that, not now. Instead she reached out to push up the hem of his T-shirt. Her fingers were remarkably steady as she unfastened his jeans, slid down the zipper then pushed the pants past his hips so that he was only left with his boxers.

He knelt down to untie his shoes and take them off, then the pants were completely gone. As if sensing she needed to undress him, he stood in front of her again and waited. Belinda got to her feet and lifted his shirt over his head. She was now up close and personal with the bare skin of the chest she'd been touching only moments ago. She didn't hesitate but touched him again, letting her fingers roam over the contours and ridges of his perfectly sculpted chest and abs.

"Damn, your touch feels so good," he whispered, his hands going to her shoulders and kneading.

His touch felt good, too; everything about this moment felt amazingly good and she couldn't wait for it to continue.

Malik removed her clothes the same way she'd done with him. He looked everywhere, his gaze making her more than a little nervous. He touched her everywhere, tweaking her nipples, sliding slowly, sinuously down her stomach to her navel, then tracing an enticing line right above the juncture of her legs.

"Perfect," he said when he was kneeling on the bed, looking at her as she lay there completely naked.

She shook her head. "No. You are perfect."

"We're going to be perfect together," was his reply when he lowered himself over her and kissed her deeply.

So deeply Belinda might have forgotten where she was or what she was doing if he hadn't slipped a hand between their bodies to part her legs. The minute his fingers separated her tender folds she hissed, spikes of pleasure rocketing through her body until her head thrashed wildly.

"God, you're so soft and so wet," he whispered against her ear before licking her lobe.

She parted her legs farther, needing whatever he was doing to go on and on until she found what she was looking for. Only, Belinda didn't really know what that was. There was a building of pressure that had her knees trembling, her breathing labored. She moaned loudly, would in any other circumstances have hated the sound, but here and now she could do nothing else.

"Malik." His name came out a strangled whisper, then his lips were on hers again.

Everything in her mind was clouded, punctuated only by his touch. His lips moved down her neck, dropping featherlight kisses on her shoulders and over the swell of her breasts. When his mouth closed over her nipple, his hand continuing to work its magic between her legs, Belinda felt an undeniable sensation inside her. It was a weightlessness that bordered on euphoria. Her own hands reached for the comforter, grabbing fistfuls as her entire body trembled and her world shifted undeniably.

She was more beautiful than he'd expected and Malik's gaze hungrily drank in the sight of her. He wanted to stop and stare, to gaze longingly, but his body had other plans. His hands were drawn to her like magnets, his mouth fused to her lips, her shoulders, her breasts, every inch of her skin. He simply could not get enough.

And when she came, the extremely tight walls of her center clenching hot and wet around his fingers, he thought he would join her in that eternal bliss. His erection throbbed painfully, pre-juices dripping from its tip.

It took monumental strength—a feat he would later revel in—to pull back only seconds after she'd trembled in his arms. She whimpered and reached for him.

"Just a second, baby. Just one second," he whispered through gritting teeth as he climbed off the bed. Finding his wallet in his back pants pocket he pulled out a condom and quickly sheathed himself. When he was once again between her legs, he couldn't help but look down. It was a mistake, he knew, but he was too weak to stop it.

The plump folds of her center glistened with arousal, and his mouth watered. She shifted, moving her legs farther apart, lifting them slightly, and he wanted to cry out. Instead he scooped her legs up in his arms and lowered his head. The minute his lips touched her moistened skin, the taste of pure honey layering his tongue, Malik moaned.

Belinda gasped, as if she hadn't expected this. He licked her longingly, slowly, and she whispered his name. It almost sounded like a question, but Malik pushed that thought aside as her hands gripped the back of his head, pushing him deeper. For what seemed like an eternity he feasted on the decadence that was Belinda. Her hips thrust forward and he held her through yet another release, this one leaving her limp beneath him.

Making his way back up to her face, he whispered into her ear, "I can't wait to feel you wrapped tightly around me. Can't wait to sink inside of you."

"Please," she said in a sated and impatient voice. "Now?"

That was definitely a question and Malik pulled back slightly to look at her. She had her eyes closed. "Open your eyes, Belinda."

She tried once and they drifted closed again.

"Belinda, open your eyes and tell me you want this, too. I won't go any further if you're having doubts." Even though he feared not going further might actually kill him, he would definitely stop if that's what she wanted.

Her head shook almost instantly. "No. Please, don't stop." When she finally opened her eyes to look at him, they were filled with desire, dark and bewitching in the muted light of the room.

He moved so that his erection was now between the folds of her center. She lifted her legs and locked them around his waist.

"I said, now," she told him thrusting her hips upward.

Malik nodded, their gazes locked, and pushed into her with one swift thrust. She screamed and he froze, blood rushing loudly in his head as realization struck him like a brick.

He opened his mouth to speak and she lifted slightly,

kissed his lips. "Now," she told him. "Right now, dammit."

Her hands had grasped his buttocks, sending spikes of pleasure down his spine, and he began to pump. Despite the thoughts running through his mind, Malik's desire took over. His body took what it had wanted for far too long. And Belinda gave. Damn, did she give. With every thrust of her hips, every grind, every whimper, she gave him exactly what he wanted, needed.

And when he'd finally found his release, when she'd screamed his name more times than he could count, he rolled off her, pulling her body close to his and finally breathed, "Why didn't you tell me?"

Chapter 8

"Tell you what?" Belinda asked as she attempted to roll away from him. Apparently that wasn't part of the sexual ritual, because Malik quickly grabbed her around the waist, pulling her backside up against his front.

"Don't do that," he said, his lips close to her ear. "Don't run. It's a little too late for that."

"I'm going to the bathroom," she replied, even though every part of her screamed for her to run as fast and as far as she possibly could.

"Belinda." He said her name as if it frustrated him. "There are a couple things I ask of women I'm involved with. One is honesty."

"What's the other?" she asked out of curiosity.

"Exclusivity, but I'm almost certain that isn't a problem with you. Especially knowing what I now know."

Belinda took a deep breath. He was right, running was not an option. It was best to deal with this situation the same way she'd dealt with all the others in her life—head-on, with the cool demeanor she was known for.

"Yes, you were my first so it's apparent I'm not the sleep-around type."

"I never would have guessed I'd be your first."

"I distinctly remember saying you don't know everything about me." She tried to move again, figuring she'd told him what he wanted to know.

"Still trying to run?"

Belinda sighed. Really, it wasn't that she was trying to run. She did have to go to the bathroom and she wanted a moment alone to really experience what they'd just done. Truth be told, it was amazing. More amazing than she had anticipated, and yet there was something she knew instinctively was missing.

"I have to go to the bathroom," she told him.

"That's fair," he said, releasing her. "I'll be here when you return."

He would. She knew it even as she decided how to hold the sheet over her body and slip from the bed. Her robe hung on the back of her bedroom door and she crossed the room quickly to obtain it, before heading to the bathroom. Malik would not slip into his clothes and leave her for the night, like she'd heard happened after many one-night stands. How she knew this about Malik, Belinda wasn't totally sure. This was a side of him she had no clue about.

By the time she'd taken care of her personal needs and resigned herself to going back out into the bedroom, she was feeling pretty damn good about her decision. She'd slept with Malik Anthony and she was happy about that.

He went into the bathroom immediately after her,

which gave her time to pick up her clothes and place them in the hamper. She folded his and put them on the lounge chair near the window. They smelled like him, strong and masculine was the scent of his cologne. Her fingers were still lingering over the material when he came out.

"You okay?" he asked.

She turned to see he was still completely naked. It was a pleasant shock, one she figured most new lovers shared. Lovers? The thought warmed her. But was that what she'd wanted out of all this? Her initial thought had just been to go for something she'd never experienced, to do something her parents would most likely disagree with, and with someone they didn't know. When she decided Malik would be the one, long term hadn't occurred to her at all. So she wasn't prepared to discuss it. That was totally unlike her.

"I'm good," was her reply.

His smile was slow and sexy and solicited the appropriate response from her now hardening nipples.

"I can now attest to that," he told her as he moved closer. "But there's something bothering you. I can tell because you get that little dimple between your brows when you're in deep thought or trying to figure something out."

Belinda purposely relaxed, hoping that dimple that she knew for a fact was there—because he was right again, dammit—would disappear.

"I have a lot on my mind what with the competition and the charity auction next weekend."

"What charity auction?" he asked as he came to stand beside her. He lifted her hands from his clothes, bringing them to his lips for a light kiss. Then he led her to the bed. He sat, pulling her down beside him.

Clearly, he was used to walking around naked. She wondered how many women had been blessed enough to see this sight. Then she forced herself to forget that thought. It was way too unsettling.

"The NAACP, or should I say Daisy Drayson-Jones's charity event of the year. My mother acts like this is her personal event."

"Yeah, I remember Drake saying something about that now. It's supposedly a really big deal. You know that congressman we did the baby shower cake for the other day? He and his wife are attending and donated some artwork for the auction."

"How do you know all that?"

Malik shook his head. "I'm a people person. People tell me all kinds of stuff," he said with a smile. "When his assistant came in to place the order, she asked if your mother was any relation to 'the' Lillian Drayson. When I told her she was, she talked even more."

"I'm sure she just wanted to keep you talking. Your people skills were probably on full blast," she said in a tone she thought sounded a little jealous. So she followed up with a little chuckle.

"Just doing the customer service thing," he replied. "So what do you have to do for the auction? Are you baking something?"

"Oh, no," she said, shaking her head. "Life couldn't be that easy. Not for me anyway. No, my mother just wants me to show up, look impeccable and have a date that looks the same."

"I see."

"No. You don't." Belinda sighed. "That's all everyone

sees is me looking impeccable. Me doing the right thing. Me being in the right place with the right person at the right time. It's to the point where I'm sick of being me!"

"Been there, done that."

His reply was said so matter-of-factly, so simply, Belinda had to look at him. "What are you talking about?"

"Everybody wanted me to be a basketball star. My mom wanted it since the first time I picked up a ball. She took me everywhere she could so I could be seen by who she thought were important people. And when she married Geoff and we moved to a better neighborhood, she figured my chances were even better. I was groomed to play in the NBA. Not that that was a bad thing. Not until one day, when I couldn't play anymore."

"That must have been hard for you," she replied honestly and felt like her own complaint may have been a bit on the selfish and immature side compared to what Malik had suffered.

"Life's hard, Belinda. I learned that when I realized I was the only kid on the block with no father in the house. When I watched my mother work two and sometimes three jobs, hustling me from one friend's house to another, all so she could keep a roof over our heads and make sure I had good shoes to play in. The key is just to keep moving."

"I keep moving. It just seems like I'm going in the same circle, though. I mean, don't get me wrong, I love what I do. I love my family and I love the bakery. I'm just afraid that at the end of the day—" She paused and put down her head.

Malik brushed back her hair, tucking it behind her ear and cupping her cheek. "What are you afraid of, Belinda?"

She looked at him and voiced the concern that had plagued her for…she wasn't sure how long.

"I'm afraid none of that stuff will ever really love me back."

His kiss this time was different. Instead of being packed with desire and passion—which were still there in small measure—it was softer, slower, as if trying to convince her of something. Belinda leaned into the kiss, let her hands fall on his shoulders in an attempt to remain steady. But that was a futile attempt as powerful as Malik's kisses seemed to be with her.

Pulling back, he rested his forehead against hers as they both struggled to catch their breath. "Stuff doesn't love you back, Belinda," he told her seriously. "But people can, if you open yourself up to receive it."

The words made sense but the concept was foreign to her. With the exception of her family, Belinda had never loved a man and never hoped a man could really love her. How could he when the woman he saw was the one she constantly pretended to be?

"It's late," Malik said, interrupting her thoughts. He was already moving, adjusting them beneath the covers that before had been ruffled by their lovemaking. "Let's get some sleep. Everything will look better in the morning."

Belinda was tired, her mind still reeling with what they'd done, wondering if there would be repercussions. As she lay back tucked snugly in Malik's arm, the side of her body pressed warmly against his, she let his words sink in. They reminded her of something her grandmother always said. *Joy will come in the morning.* Belinda hoped so, because for too long, joy seemed to have purposely evaded her.

Chapter 9

Belinda bolted straight up in the bed, her heart beating wildly, panic streaking through her body in stinging waves.

Beside her, Malik touched her arm. "What is it? Are you okay?"

She shook her head, scrambling across the bed in an attempt to get away from him.

He caught her by wrapping one strong arm around her waist, the other touching her shoulder, holding her still. "Belinda, calm down. It's me, Malik."

The sound of his voice, his name, and memories of their time together came flooding back. Yesterday she'd spent the entire day with Malik Anthony, watching him coach his young basketball team. It had been a day full of laughter and touching moments.

Then they'd come back to her place, she and Malik.

He'd touched her and she'd felt empowered. She'd touched him and then…

And after all that, he was still here. The morning after, Malik was in her bed, once again holding her securely, safely.

She took a deep breath, let it out slowly and repeated the action again and again, until her heart slowed to a somewhat normal rhythm. The panic attack had come on quickly, sitting on her chest like a lead weight, threatening to smother her completely. But why? she thought, quickly looking around her room.

Everything looked the same. The two windows on the wall opposite the door were closed, locked. Her television was turned off, the lights, as well. The bathroom door was open because she wasn't a big fan of closed doors besides the front one that should be locked and bolted. Her gaze dropped immediately to her alarm clock, her heart rate picking up slightly.

"It's late," she whispered.

His chin grazed her shoulder, warmth brushing her ear as he spoke. "No. It's not. Your normal arrival time at the bakery is seven-thirty. It's a quarter to six. The ride to work is about fifteen minutes from here."

She was shaking her head. "My alarm is always set to go off at five-fifteen. I always get up at five-fifteen."

He'd wrapped his arms around her now, holding her completely still.

"I turned it off. We were up so late last night, I thought you'd need all the sleep you could get before work this morning. It's okay, baby. You won't be late."

His voice was so soft, so controlled. She didn't understand why. If she was late getting up, he should be frantic, too, since he was also due at the bakery at seven.

"But we have orders and we'll be late."

"Shari's on the early shift this week, Belinda. We can go in at seven-thirty and everything will be fine."

"But—"

He cut her off by turning her slightly, taking her lips with his. Of course she couldn't think with him kissing her. And of course her heart rate calmed as she was getting used to his voice and his touch. But still…

There was no time for *buts* as his kiss deepened and she fell slowly, irrevocably into Malik's arms.

"Sweet, sexy Belinda," he whispered softly before dropping light kisses down her neck until his lips once again found her breasts.

She loved the feel of his hands on each breast, the tightness with which he grabbed each once, squeezing until her nipples were rock hard. Then his mouth was over one nipple, his teeth grabbing the turgid bud and holding on tight, but not painfully so. Then his tongue took over, licking around her nipple, along the side swell of her breast and back to the nipple again.

Belinda's breath now came in heavy pants as her fingers gripped his shoulders. Her center throbbed and ached.

Malik focused on her other breast now, soliciting a moan of approval from Belinda. When his other arm slid down her back to grip her bottom, she whispered his name. "Malik."

"Yes, baby. I'm right here."

And she was oh so glad he was here, right at this moment, doing exactly what he was doing.

When his hand came from around her buttocks to touch her tender folds she almost leaped off the bed, but he held her still. "I know, baby. It feels so good, doesn't it?"

"Yes," she whimpered uncontrollably.

Everything he did felt good, every touch, every whisper... Dammit, his lips were no longer on her breasts. Malik had slid down her body so slowly, so seamlessly, Belinda had barely noticed. But now that he had both her legs scooped in his arms and had lowered his face so that his warm breath was blowing directly over that tightened nub of her center, she wanted to scream.

He licked that tight nub and she shivered all over. Another lick, then he sucked it completely into his mouth and the scream escaped. To hell with her neighbors and how early it was in the morning. She thought about being embarrassed by how loud she was, or how her legs shook as she panted, but she couldn't. The sensations rippling through her at this moment were too intense to focus on anything else.

By the time Malik had once again sheathed his thick length and sank slowly into her waiting moistness, Belinda's bones were so limp, her body so on fire for him she could have spontaneously combusted right at that moment.

This was slower and infinitely more potent than the quick, heated lovemaking they'd shared last night. His hips rocked against hers, planting him deeper, firmer into her center until Belinda began to feel like she'd been born with him just like this, connected to her forevermore.

"You feel so hot, so damn sexy, so right," Malik murmured finally in her ear.

"So do you," she admitted with her chin resting on his shoulder, her face thankfully facing away from him.

He felt good in her arms, so strong and toned, and he was here with her. Belinda was still having a hard time digesting that fact. Meanwhile she held on tight while he thrust deeper, pulled out then sank back in again. He filled her so completely, so thoroughly, and she enjoyed it. More than she could have ever possibly imagined.

"It seems like I've waited forever to have you like this," Malik told her when he'd pulled back to look down at her, all the while still working his hips.

Belinda had no idea how he could concentrate on conversation at a time like this. Perspiration had begun to sheen their bodies even though they were moving slowly. Her breath was steady but still irregular. She wanted to close her eyes and focus only on the feeling of him, their connection, and what she would do when he finally left.

"Look at me, Belinda. Don't think. Just look at me and feel," he told her, leaning his face so close to hers his breath whispered along her damp skin.

She opened her eyes, stared directly into his and felt everything around her spiral out of control. "Malik," she murmured.

"That's right. It's me. And you. We're together and damn, it feels good."

That was no lie. As a matter of fact, the sentiment should have been carved into a statue because she was almost certain sex would get no better than this.

"Yes," she whispered. "It feels good."

As if he were waiting for those words Malik's entire body tensed over hers. Then his slow thrusts picked up pace as he pounded into her. At first glance it would seem like the abrupt change of pace would be problematic. How very untrue. Belinda arched off the bed, moving her hips to match his rhythm, then Malik pulled one of her legs up to rest on his shoulder, letting him plunge even deeper into her. Yes, she thought, sex with Malik Anthony was one hell of a ride.

One Belinda hated to get off. But reality would almost always sink in.

Hours later, when Belinda was in her element—in the kitchen at the bakery—she pushed memories of the night and this morning with Malik out of her mind.

He'd thankfully been scarce around the bakery this morning. She actually hadn't seen him since he'd left her apartment at six-thirty to head back to his place to change. It was now a little after eleven and she and Shari were the only ones in the kitchen. Belinda mixed batches of lemon pound-cake batter, which would make the poppy-seed pound cake that was a customer favorite, while Shari rolled out dough for the different-flavored turnovers for tomorrow. Much of their work was prep for the next day, as the bulk of the orders going out today were Carter's. Any walk-ins would be handled by Shari and Belinda, while Malik had spent most of his time in the showroom, or at least that's where Belinda suspected he was.

"I've laid out some plans for the competition," Shari said, snapping Belinda out of her reverie.

"What? Strategic plans?"

"Yes. The theme is Around the World, so I've broken the different countries up and figured we could all specialize in one area, so we're not spreading ourselves too thin. I have some design sketches I did over the weekend. We need to buckle down and get a game plan going, then start practicing. We have got to win this."

Shari hadn't looked up from rolling her dough but her voice seemed a little tense. "I agree this is an important competition, but I don't think we need to obsess over it," Belinda said slowly.

"What? Who's obsessing? I'm just stating the facts. If we're going to beat Dina and Brown Sugar Bakery, we've got to have our stuff together. Totally."

"I agree," Belinda said. "But, Shari, I think we need to separate the business from the personal here. I mean, what happened with Dina was years ago."

"Unfortunately, time does not erase the past," was Shari's reply.

"No, that's why it's up to us to move on. To leave the past in the past," she told her cousin seriously.

Dina's betrayal had obviously hit Shari the hardest. Everyone in the family had felt hurt and angry by Dina's action, but for the most part, Belinda thought they'd all moved on. At least she knew she had. Dina had taught them a valuable lesson about keeping their family recipes and traditions a secret. Malik had actually been the only other person not blood related that was privy to the inner workings of Lillian's.

"That's easy for you to say," Shari retorted, looking up now from her work.

Belinda was startled at her cousin's sharp words. "What's that supposed to mean?"

"It means that if you would come out of your self-made glass house every now and then and live a little you might have a past and something you regret doing."

This wasn't the first time Shari, or anyone for that matter, had made a remark about Belinda living in a glass house. The saying definitely was not true. If it were, she'd have shattered the walls of that so-called perfect life of hers a long time ago.

"Believe me, I have plenty of regrets," she said solemnly as she began scooping batter from the bowl, layering it gently into the loaf pans.

"You? Yeah, right. What do you regret? Getting your hair cut too short or maybe buying the wrong shoes to go with an outfit? You don't have any regrets, Belinda, because you don't ever take chances. You make the right choice each and every time. The safe choice, I should say."

To admit she was offended by that accusation would be an understatement even though some of it may have been true. Belinda had taken the easy route; she'd done what everyone expected of her all the time, instead of doing what she wanted. As a result she was living a life that was mostly a lie. And that didn't sit well with her.

"You're right," she said simply. "I'm trying to get better at that."

Shari was prepared to go on stating her case, which was so like her. If you wanted in your corner a loyal person who was honest to a fault, it would be Shari. Belinda didn't resent her cousin for that. In fact, she admitted, if only to herself, she was sort of envious of her for it.

"Trying to get better at what? And did you just say I was right?" Shari asked. Once again, she looked up at Belinda. "Wait a minute," she said, dropping the cutter she used to fashion perfect triangles from the dough and coming from around the table where she worked.

Belinda shifted slightly as Shari came to stand beside her.

"What's going on with you? And don't bother to tell me nothing because I know you better than that."

Shari was oh so right. They knew each other very well, since they'd all grown up on Lillian's estate. It had seemed strange that all of Lillian's children had remained living on her estate for so many years after they were grown and married. But that could only be attributed to how close their family was, in and out of the business.

"Nothing's going on. I'm fine," she said, knowing damn well Shari was going to keep pushing until Belinda told her the absolute truth. With that in mind Belinda gave up before Shari could continue. "Okay, but this goes no farther than this kitchen."

"What did you do? Something illegal? Did you kill that bastard Patrick for calling you stuck-up?"

"What? No, girl. You watch too much television."

"Please, Andre is addicted to the cartoon network, so I'm not seeing much about murders these day. But whatever, go on and tell me what you did."

"I didn't do anything." Belinda sighed, then smiled. "Well, I did sort of do something."

Shari tilted her head, staring intently at Belinda. "And that something was…?"

Belinda cleared her throat. "I had sex."

Shari took a step back. "Is that all?"

Of course Shari didn't know that Belinda had never had sex before. It wasn't something she'd eagerly broadcasted. In fact, she'd been guarding that little secret with her entire being for as long as she could remember. And there was no doubt that Shari wasn't in the same boat since Andre would be turning five in about seven months. No wonder it didn't sound like much to her.

"With Malik," she said quickly, then turned her attention back to scooping out the cake batter.

Shari's hands were on her shoulders turning her around so fast Belinda dripped cake batter all over the table.

"Leave it," Shari ordered. "Tell me everything. Don't leave out one little detail and don't try to tell me you don't remember. Your mind is like a steel trap. If y'all did it, you remember it. Now spill."

Belinda felt like they were teenagers again. With both of them in their mid-twenties it wasn't that far of a stretch.

"I helped out at his fund-raiser yesterday and, when we came back to my apartment, things got a little heated and we…we did it." She shrugged like it was as simple as that, which was definitely not true.

"You and Malik? Carter's friend Malik and you?"

"Is that so hard to believe?"

"Aah, yes, it is hard to believe. He's not the type you ordinarily go out with."

Belinda reached for a cloth and went to the sink to wet it. "You're telling me something I already know. But that doesn't have to be a bad thing. Maybe my tastes are changing."

"Maybe," Shari said, still eyeing her suspiciously. "Or maybe you've had a thing for him all along and just chose to finally act on it."

"That sounds impulsive and more of an act that would suit Carter, not me," Belinda said.

"Carter wouldn't have sex with his best friend." Shari shook her head and chuckled as Belinda cleaned up the spilled cake batter from the table.

Belinda eyed her over her shoulder. "You know what I mean."

"Okay, so let's say you're straying from the norm.

Fine, there's no problem with sampling different items before you settle on one. I probably should have done a little more sampling myself before…" Shari cleared her throat. "So what does that mean for the two of you now?"

"Nothing," Belinda answered quickly. Too quickly.

"Uh-huh, that was really believable. Are you a couple? Is it serious? Are you in love with him?"

"Are you a cop hanging out in this kitchen as an undercover disguise?" Belinda asked her cousin, who was like a pit bull when she sank her teeth in something.

Shari shook her head. She wore her hair pulled back today, as she normally did when she was in the kitchen, and she had on jeans and a T-shirt—also her normal "mommy" clothes and "bakery" clothes when she wasn't meeting with clients. She was shorter than Belinda, with more curves and a round face that displayed high cheekbones when she smiled.

"I told myself I'm not going to overthink this situation. I'm going to simply go with the flow."

Shari laughed.

"What?"

"You? Go with the flow? That doesn't even sound right coming out of your mouth. You don't go with the flow, Belinda. You make the flow, you control the ups and the downs and you make it work for you. That's who you are."

Belinda shook her head. "That's not who I want to be. I thought I was controlling everything with all the other dates I've been on and you see how they turned out. I just want to relax and let things happen naturally. And if it doesn't work out, that's fine." Because really, she'd only considered Malik as a man she trusted to have sex with. It had never really dawned on her there could be something more between them. At least not until he said he'd waited so long for her. That little comment still had her head spinning.

"So you wouldn't commit to Malik if that's what he wanted?"

"That's not what he wants," she replied adamantly.

"How do you know? Did you ask him?"

"Have you seen Malik with a steady girlfriend in all the years we've known him? I haven't. He's just like Carter in that respect, not in it for the long run."

"I don't know about that," Shari said. "There are some distinct differences between Carter and Malik. And anyway we aren't talking about you sleeping with your cousin. We're talking about you sleeping with a fine, intelligent man who has his priorities straight and a bright future ahead of him."

"I know Malik's attributes. You don't have to rattle them off like you're his personal résumé."

Shari folded her hands over her chest and leaned a hip against the table. Belinda dropped the spoon and drummed her nails on the stainless steel.

"He's not my type, I know this. But he said he'd wanted me for a long time. He touched me and I melted. I liked that. So that's it, right?"

Shari shook her head. "Doesn't sound like that's it to me. Let me give you some advice. I think you should date Malik, sleep with him as much as you want, protected of course, and see where it ends up. Because I guarantee you one thing—if you give up on this relationship before it's had a chance to grow, you'll regret it for the rest of your life."

Shari seemed deadly serious about her words. So

much so Belinda had to wonder if she weren't speaking from her own experience, perhaps with Andre's father. She was wise enough and respectful enough of her cousin's privacy not to ask her that question. Instead she nodded, agreeing that she should at least think about the possibility of Malik being the man for her.

Belinda Drayson-Jones, twenty-six-year-old beautiful and intelligent pastry chef, was a virgin. Or at least she had been before last night. Before he'd taken something from her that she would never get back.

A part of Malik had walked to his car this morning with his chest poked out and his ego significantly inflated. Another part, the one that had taken over the minute he stepped foot into the bakery an hour later, was beginning to feel more than a little regretful.

"Hiding out?" Carter said from behind him just as Malik finished filling an order of three cheesecakes and two of Belinda's famous Key Lime Pies.

"I'm working. You do remember that, don't you?" he asked, since it was almost noon and Carter was just coming in.

Carter grinned, his world-class "I'm Carter Drayson and who the hell are you" grin. "I know very well what work is. That's why I'm here to work on that carnival cake for the Children's Hospital. But what I'm more curious about is why you're out here instead of in the back."

"Shari and Belinda are prepping for tomorrow. All the orders on the books are yours. Three of them are ready—after your final approval that is—to be shipped. And the carnival cake, you still need to decorate. That leaves me to man the store."

"Where's Amber?"

"Dentist's appointment."

Carter shook his head. "Convenient excuse."

Malik closed the display case, mentally making note of what was left and what he'd need to retrieve from the back to stock up. The last thing they wanted, even though it meant they were making good sales, was for a customer to come in and see an empty display case. As Lillian would say, *That was classless.*

"For?" he asked, moving around Carter, who was rudely standing directly in his path.

"For the fact that you're hiding from Belinda."

Malik stopped near the second display case and turned to face Carter. "Why would I hide from your cousin?"

Carter shrugged and the look he gave Malik was one of innocent ignorance, except his grin shifted to over-bearing arrogance.

"Heard you were together yesterday. All day," Carter told him. He'd moved across the showroom to the coffee bar. Nichelle, who'd been with them since the installation of the bar, immediately served him a cappuccino.

"How could you possibly have heard that?"

"Lorielle Simmons sent me a text. She saw that you and Belinda were at the rec center and wondered why I hadn't come to represent the bakery."

Lorielle Simmons was one of Carter's many conquests, who happened to be the daughter of an NCAA college coach. She was also one of the biggest supporters of Malik's foundation. And apparently she could now be classified as a snitch.

"She wanted to help, that's all," Malik replied.

Carter nodded as he sipped his drink. "Right, I know all about how your women help you out."

Malik frowned.

"But let me just tell you something I forgot to mention the other day when you asked how I felt about you pursuing Belinda."

"And what studious advice should I be forever grateful to you for?"

Carter sobered instantly, his brown eyes darkening. "Hurt my cousin and I'll kick your ass."

He should have expected that. Actually, he'd been looking forward to a remark like that when he'd first told Carter about his intentions toward Belinda. Carter was very protective of his family, of his female cousins especially. No matter how bossy and irritating Belinda could sometimes be to him, he wasn't about to let anything happen to her. Or, as he'd just said, let anybody hurt her.

"You know me better than that," Malik replied.

"I know women fall in love with your quiet charm, your big ole compassionate heart. So all I'm saying is tread lightly with Belinda. We've been friends for a long time and we've been through a lot. The last thing I want to have to do is hit you."

"First," Malik said, folding his arms over his chest, "you've hit me before and we both ended up with black eyes and sore ribs the next morning—courtesy of a bad bet on my part and too many rum and cokes on your part.

"And second, you've got me confused with you. I don't leave a trail of broken hearts beating behind me. I'm much more discreet in my conquests."

Carter shrugged. "Either way, I felt it my duty to warn you."

"Right. Thanks for that," Malik added drily. "Anything else you want to say?"

"Only that one of your discreet conquests just walked through the door."

Malik turned to the front door just as he heard Carter's mocking laugh heading into the back.

Chantelle Martin wanted to be one of his conquests, discreet or any other way she could. Malik didn't like her blatant sexuality or the way she flaunted it, even in the presence of her children. She wore gaudy makeup and extremely tight clothes. Her voice was loud and her eyes were way too big for her face. She took care of her sons on her own because their fathers were mysteriously—or not—out of the picture. She worked two jobs and was apparently so good at both she still made it to the boys' games.

But she wasn't Belinda.

"Hello, Malik," Chantelle said, stopping in front of the second display case.

She wore a red dress that was snug over her hips and breasts. Cleavage was bountiful, and legs should have been in their own display case.

"Hello, Chantelle. What brings you into Lillian's today? Do you need a cake or a pie? Or do you just want more of my Belgian chocolate brownies?"

Chantelle leaned over the counter and extended her arm until her nails ran over his shoulder. "I'll take all of the above if you'll personally deliver them to my place around seven-thirty tonight."

"I can have them boxed and ready for you to take out in three minutes," he said seriously.

She smiled, licking her tongue over glossed lips. "I want door-to-door service. Doesn't Lillian care anything about customer service?"

Malik nodded. "It's number one in our book."

"Then good customer service would demand you deliver the items personally, wouldn't it?"

"Only if you bought out the entire store," Belinda said from the doorway, where Malik was surprised to see her standing.

She barely looked at him as she walked to the display case, a gorgeous smile on her face while she stared at Chantelle. "Is that an option, Ms., or is it Mrs., Martin?"

"It's Mrs. Martin," Chantelle said, her tone quickly turning frosty. "I have no need for the contents of the entire store. But I would like my order delivered."

"Sure," Belinda told her and reached around Malik to grab the delivery log. She passed Mrs. Martin a slip of paper and said, "Fill this out and we'll get your delivery ready."

Malik stood back watching as Belinda waited on Chantelle with style and finesse even though annoyance almost radiated from her. He could tell by the way she tapped the pen against the log then tucked the shorter side of her hair behind her ear. That was a true sign that she was angry and couldn't show it.

When Mrs. Martin passed her the paper with all her information on it, she looked over to Malik. "If you're available I'd like you to deliver it. If not, I'd like you to call me when you are."

"Carlos is our new delivery guy. He's fantastic. I'll tell him to make sure he delivers only to you," Belinda said, then gave Malik one of the sharpest, coldest looks he'd ever received.

He cleared his throat and stepped closer. "She's right. Carlos is great. He'll make sure you have everything on your order and on time, first thing Saturday morning," he said after looking in the log book where Belinda had just written down the information.

Chantelle's lips closed tightly, her gaze never wavering from him. "That will be fine," she said. "For now."

She walked out of the store with a deliberate sway of her hips. Her perfume loomed seconds after she was gone.

"Big order?" he asked.

"Big jerk!" Belinda said, pushing past him to head back into the kitchen.

Chapter 10

Belinda had a headache. As she took two aspirin and washed them down with cran-grape juice, she sighed. A headache was much better than a panic attack. Today had been a long day. Ten and a half hours at the bakery, including a last-minute change in cake design coming just ten minutes after she'd finished the cake, her touch-and-go conversation with Shari and last but certainly not least, the run-in with Malik and his flavor of the month.

Rubbing her throbbing temples, Belinda sat on her couch and let her head fall back, eyes closed.

The decision to sleep with Malik had been an impulsive one. She hadn't thought it through, hadn't considered all the consequences and repercussions. But she had enjoyed it immensely. And that had been her ultimate goal. Only now, even that felt kind of hollow. As far as changing her life went, Belinda realized she sucked. Her old habits kept getting in the way. Sitting here thinking about Malik instead of being out changing things with Malik was just one example of how hard it was to kick old habits.

As if the heavens heard her thoughts, the doorbell rang. Belinda got up from the couch, walked slowly toward the door. It was her practice to look through the peephole first. If she recognized her visitor, she'd then wait for the second ring to see how persistent they were about seeing her. Next, she would— It didn't matter. The peep through the hole showed her just the man that had been occupying her thoughts.

How lucky was that?

"Hey," he said the moment she opened the door. "Dressed for bed at—" Malik paused and twisted his wrist to look at his watch "—at eight-thirty. Man, you're early."

"And you're uninvited," was her immediate, if not intentionally nasty, reply.

Shaking his head, Malik moved past her into the apartment. He waited for her to close the door then took a step closer, backing her against the door.

"I see I'm going to have to go over the rules with you one more time," he told her.

"What rules?" Belinda asked, inhaling the scent of his cologne as he blocked out everything else around her, physically and literally.

"The rules of a relationship." His words were punctuated by the quick smack of his lips against hers.

"Mmmmm," he moaned, then went in for kiss number two.

This one wasn't quick and Belinda couldn't resist. She let his lips cover hers, parted her own and enjoyed the feel of his tongue brushing alongside her own. The feeling was familiar—the spike of arousal that arrowed through her as their kiss deepened. When her hands went to his chest, that too felt familiar. His strength pressed against her, his body filling a space that for too long had surrounded her.

"First rule," he said, breathing heavily as he finally tore away his mouth from hers. "Greeting kisses like that are always required."

Not that she was arguing the act of kissing him, but Belinda frowned. "I've never heard of rules in a relationship."

He took her hand and turned, pulling her the short distance from the door to the couch before sitting them both down.

"That's because you've never been in a relationship with me."

"True enough," she admitted.

He sat right next to her, his arm going around her like this was their spot. It was silly, she knew, but it was a very comfortable spot, either way.

"Another rule is the sharing thing. I don't share," Malik told her seriously.

Tonight he wore all black, jeans—of course—and a T-shirt that looked as if it were a second skin. His pectorals and biceps bulged to the point that her mouth was going to start watering if she didn't stop staring at him. He looked sexy and intense and…sexy.

"Selfish, are we?" she asked with a grin, trying to lighten the mood that had turned suddenly serious at his words.

"Absolutely. Especially when it comes to you. So

while we're seeing each other, we're not seeing anyone else."

"Like Mrs. Martin for instance?"

How dare he come in here and start laying out rules when he was the one flirting with the basketball mom with more breasts and hips than she knew what to do with.

"What?"

He actually looked shocked for a moment. Then he smiled, slow and sexy.

"There's nothing going on between me and Mrs. Martin."

"I couldn't tell earlier today, or yesterday for that matter."

"She's the mother of one of my players. I don't mix business with pleasure."

"Is that so? Then what's this between us?" She couldn't believe she'd asked him that. Belinda knew what this was. It was a step toward freedom, her long-overdue entrance into the adult world. That was the plan, or at least she thought that should have been the plan—if she'd had one in the first place.

"What you saw was me being nice."

"No," was her adamant reply. "What I saw was you doing what too many men do. You sucked up the praise, let your ego be inflated by this woman's interest then played like it didn't affect you. You're leading her on and you should stop it."

"Wow, you even analyze flirting."

He said it like that was a bad thing.

"I'm just saying that it's kind of rude of you not to simply tell her you're not interested. I mean, unless you are interested and are playing some hard-to-get game with her. Which I don't think is the case. She's really not your type."

"And what is my type? Since you're so busy analyzing everything."

He'd moved his arm from around her and Belinda tried not to be affected by the act. It didn't matter, she told herself.

"Flamboyant and overzealous isn't your style. It goes against your calm personality. You're much more for the sweet, understated female, the one who's pretty but doesn't use that to get her way. She has to be smart—not in how she tries to snag you—but intelligent enough to hold conversations with you and not make a fool of herself."

"Is that all? Because you seem to know exactly what I need."

"I didn't say that." And she wasn't liking his tone all of a sudden.

"And I didn't say that I was interested in Mrs. Martin. In fact, I distinctly told you I wasn't."

"And I believe you."

He nodded. "Good. I'm glad I've gotten your stamp of approval."

"What is your problem?" she asked finally, fed up and coming to stand in front of him.

"My problem is you and this act you feel obligated to put on. If you were jealous because you saw me with Mrs. Martin, just say that."

"I was not jealous!" Okay, maybe just a little bit.

His raised brow said he hadn't believed her anyway.

"It's a human reaction, Belinda."

"Yeah, if you're in love with someone and deeply

committed to them. That's not what we are or where we are. We just…just…"

"We just what? Had sex? Is that what you're about to say?"

He was standing now, too, tension sizzling through the room like lightning.

She opened her mouth then clamped it shut. They needed some space, she thought. Stepping back she took a deep breath and released it. "Yes, Malik, we had sex. If I had known it would change things like this—"

"You mean you didn't know? You didn't calculate the odds and map out your course? Did you figure we'd have sex then go back to being coworkers the next day?"

"Yes. No. I mean… You're twisting things around." And making her headache substantially worse.

The phone rang and Belinda wanted to sigh with relief. Instead she moved past him, her shoulder bumping into his arm, as he wasn't inclined to move out of her way.

"Hello?" she just about yelled into the phone.

"Tone, Belinda. You have to always be aware of your tone."

Instead of sighing with relief she wanted to scream with impatience. Her mother had been calling her cell phone all day and Belinda had been ignoring her. She knew what Daisy's question would be and didn't want to hear it.

"Hello, Mother," she said through clenched teeth, her tone significantly lowered.

"I've been calling all day to find out if you've had a chance to find a dress."

"I already have something to wear to the auction. I thought I told you that already."

"But you didn't tell me what it was."

Because it was none of her business.

"I'm old enough to select my own clothes, Mother." Okay, that was good, even if it wasn't exactly what she wanted to say. *Take a stand,* she repeated to herself.

"I'm sure you are. I just want to know that everything is taken care of. Now, how about your date?"

"We also talked about my date the other day at lunch." With those words she remembered she wasn't alone and turned her back to Malik.

"Well, the least you can tell me is his name. Where does he work? Who are his parents?"

"Not now, Mother. I really have a headache."

"It's stress. You need to go to bed early or you'll have frown lines in the morning and wrinkles in five years."

"It's not stress," Belinda said, even though it probably was. Her mother just wouldn't want to hear that she was part of the cause of the stress Belinda carried around like luggage.

"Don't argue, Belinda. You need to get some rest. Just give me your date's name and I'll let you go."

"I'm not telling you his name." Because Belinda didn't even know it. The headache was growing into a full-body ache at this moment and she reached a hand around to the back of her neck to massage the tense muscles there.

"You're being difficult."

"I'm not. I just don't feel good right now. I'll call you tomorrow."

"I'll stop by the bakery tomorrow. We can have lunch."

Oh, Lord, please no.

"That's not good. I have plans already. I'll just call

you tomorrow. Okay, say hello to Daddy for me," Belinda said and disconnected the call.

Her heart hammered wildly in her chest as she stared down at the phone and realized what she'd just done. It was liberating and terrifying at the same time. Had she just hung up on her mother?

"It's okay. You don't have to let her control every aspect of your life," Malik said from behind her.

She spun around, her mouth open and about to reply.

Malik held up a hand. "Don't tell me I don't know what I'm talking about. I've watched your parents manipulate you for years now. I know exactly how good they are at it, and I'm telling you it's okay not to bend."

"I just don't feel like dealing with it right now. I have a headache."

"And I barged in and made it worse."

"No," she said. Actually, for a few minutes that he'd been there it had been better. "You're fine. I probably do just need some rest."

Malik shook his head. "That's your mother talking. What you need to do is have some dinner and let whatever is bothering you go until another time. You don't have to figure everything out, or know the answer instantaneously."

She narrowed her gaze at him, then turned to put the phone back on the base. "How do you always know what's going on in my head?"

He smiled then, as if the argument they'd been having previously was completely forgotten. "It's magic," he told her.

Later, much later, Belinda would think his words were absolutely true.

* * *

Pissed off did not begin to describe how Malik felt the moment she'd told him what he should have known she was thinking. What they'd shared last night was just sex.

If Belinda really assumed that, if she for one moment thought he was going to take that excuse and run with it, she wasn't half as smart as people believed.

He'd been ready to grab her and shake some sense into her when the phone rang. Divine intervention, he would later call it. In those moments she'd been speaking to her mother Malik had a chance to calm himself. Not completely, but enough to understand why she would think the way she did. It was as if she were programmed to downplay anything that she really wanted, and driven to do the things everyone else expected. Hence the way she had dodged her mother's questioning instead of just saying what she wanted to say and getting off the phone. In fact, he figured she'd been dodging her mother's calls for a while and had been caught off guard since they'd been arguing and picked up the phone unintentionally this time.

That was all well and good. Malik liked Daisy Drayson-Jones. He liked her husband, as well. But that didn't mean he had to like the way they always tried to pull their daughter's strings.

"I didn't know you could cook," she said when they were sitting at her dining room table, bowls of fettuccine Alfredo and Caesar salads in front of them.

"I'm a bachelor who doesn't like to eat fast food all the time. It was imperative that I learn how to cook. Besides, I took culinary classes, remember?"

Belinda nodded, her mouth full of the noodles and

sauce he'd cooked. Since this was her first bite, Malik waited for her reaction.

She rolled her eyes. "This is really good."

He smiled, his ego inflating another notch. Funny how, no matter what Mrs. Martin or women of her ilk said or did to him, he wasn't in the least affected. But the moment Belinda gave an inch and complimented him for something, his chest poked out proudly like the proverbial peacock.

"It would have been better if we could eat in front of the television. We're missing the reruns of *Big Bang Theory*," he told her.

"I cannot eat sitting on a couch," she replied. "Besides, that Sheldon character is annoying."

Malik nodded at that comment. He figured that's the one character on the highly rated sitcom Belinda would have a problem with. Sheldon was the obsessive-compulsive character who generally annoyed all his friends with his weird rules and outlandish requests, even though he was a brilliant scientist. The similarities, after he thought about it a moment, between Belinda and this character were uncanny.

"He is what he is. His friends know that and accept it."

"He's rigid and controlling."

She stopped the minute she said that last word. "And I am not like him!"

"I didn't say you were." Malik looked down at his food, trying unsuccessfully to hold in his smile.

"I just don't like to eat on the couch."

"And you don't like the magazines on your coffee table out of alphabetical order. You also keep your wineglass on your left-hand side even though you're right-handed. And you hate for your food to touch."

"So now I'm OCD? I'm some neurotic freak that everybody hates to be around?" She didn't sound angry, just like she wanted to really know if that's what he thought about her.

Malik shook his head. "Not at all. You are Belinda Lorraine Drayson-Jones, executive pastry chef at Lillian's. And I wouldn't change a thing about you."

That wasn't what she'd expected him to say. Malik could tell by the way her mouth opened then closed immediately without a reply. The rest of their meal proceeded in almost silence, then he convinced her to at least take their newly filled glasses of white wine into her bedroom. She'd been hesitant until he'd said, "Come on, take a walk on the wild side." The follow-up had been a huge grin on his part and a slow chuckle on hers.

"It's not going to kill me," she said more to herself than to him, and Malik decided to at least carry the glasses to make the adjustment a little easier on her.

Once they were in the bedroom, he knew that Belinda was expecting sex. Her eyes had grown darker as she'd taken a seat on the edge of the bed. And for as sexy as she was and as willing a participant as he would normally be, Malik decided that tonight was about something else.

"What's your favorite form of relaxation?" he asked.

She blinked, clearly startled at the question, before answering, "A hot bath or a good book."

He nodded. "One I can do, the other you'd have to hit the library for."

Without another word he was up and moving into her bathroom, where he immediately began running bathwater. On the stand across the daintily decorated room he saw several bottles of bubble bath, all of them a different fragrance. He decided to select one that he liked, which meant he had to smell them all. With each sniff his erection grew harder. Each scent reminded him of Belinda in a different way—naked and pliant beneath him, that was the jasmine; in the kitchen working, her tight little bottom outlined perfectly in her pants, that was the lavender; sitting quietly, daydreaming as he hadn't seen her do often enough, that was the chamomile. They all represented one woman, the one Malik was almost positive he was in love with.

He poured the lavender into the running water and went to get Belinda.

"I don't need you to run me a bath," she was saying as he ushered her inside the bathroom.

"I know you don't need me to. I want to."

She squirmed beneath his touch as Malik reached for the hem of her shirt. It was a cute little move on her part that made her breasts jiggle and him moan inwardly.

"I can definitely undress myself."

"But where's the fun in that?" he joked with a raise of his eyebrows.

His fingers brushed along the skin of her stomach as he lifted the shirt up and over her head. She was still giving him a mock pout when he traced a finger along the brim of her bra over the soft swells of her breast.

"See, this is fun," he told her, his voice noticeably lower.

"Right." She nodded, her lips twitching with a smile.

Her skin was so soft and so creamy-looking. Malik's mouth watered with wanting to kiss her there, anywhere.

"Do I get to undress you in return?" she asked when he'd finally reached behind her and unsnapped her bra.

Her breasts sprung free, her nipples already perking at his perusal.

"No," he answered simply. "Not this time."

"That's not fair," she added with a little pout.

He couldn't resist. Malik touched a fingertip to her bottom lip. "You are so sexy you're dangerous."

Unfastening her pants and pushing them over her slender hips was also a pleasure and he found his face up close with her enticing thighs. Malik kept his lips tight, refusing to give in to the urge to kiss her there, lick her possibly. She'd been wearing slippers when he arrived so it was simple enough to push them off her feet and encourage her to step out of her pants.

She held on to his shoulders while she did, her touch sending bolts of heat throughout his body. Malik stood then, left her standing in only her bikini underwear and moved to turn off the water. Fragrant bubbles were about to run over the lip of the tub and he inhaled deeply the lavender scent. She probably needed chamomile tonight, to truly soothe her and take her into a dreamless sleep. But since he wasn't going to push the physical act of lovemaking with her, Malik figured he at least needed to leave with the scent on her body, the thought in his mind, so he would have a perfectly wonderful sleep filled with sexy dreams of her.

Before he could turn back to Belinda he saw that she'd removed her own panties. He smiled at her, shaking his head. "You are so insubordinate."

She shrugged. "Just trying to help."

He nodded and reached for her hand. "Thanks a lot."

Helping her into the tub, watching her sleek body

sink slowly beneath the cover of bubbles made Malik rock hard. His entire body screamed for release, one he knew would not be coming anytime soon.

"Will you stay and talk to me?" she asked, her voice more fragile than he'd ever heard before.

"Of course. I have to wash you."

She sank into the water until the bubbles touched her chin and gave him a very dreamy, very delicious look before whispering, "Of course."

Chapter 11

Malik's hands were heaven as they finished the last circle over her back where he applied her lotion.

To add to her list of firsts, probably right at the top, Belinda would add *being bathed by a man*. No, that didn't quite describe the experience. *Being bathed by Malik* was more like it. Every place he touched sent shivers throughout her body, even now after she'd finished in the bathroom and lay across her bed, covers pulled down and waiting for her to slip beneath.

The heat of the water and the relaxing of her tired muscles had her barely able to keep her eyes open. Yet she didn't want to miss a moment of what Malik planned to do to her next.

He'd slipped the shortest nightie he could find in her drawer over her head, smoothing it down the length of her body. And now she lay there on the bed, her body completely pliant, her eyes closing and slowly reopening. His hands rubbed her shoulders and down her arms. Belinda heard herself moan but floated somewhere between heaven and earth.

When his lips touched her ear, she sighed. The kiss was chaste, the ensuing lick of his tongue like fire. She gripped her pillow tighter, sinking down into the soft bedding and loving the feel of his heat above her.

"We're not just having sex, Belinda. That's for people who don't know what they want. I know without a doubt that I want more from you," he whispered.

His voice was so sexy, so warm against her skin. His words heady enough to make her feel even more tranquil than she already did. All she could do was moan in response.

"And you can tell your mother that I'll be escorting you to the auction. Remember, I do not share."

A smile ghosted her lips, she felt it, but she did not open her eyes. His words echoed in her mind.

He didn't want to share her. Malik Anthony wanted her all to himself. And he knew exactly who she was, all her faults and everything. Yes, Belinda continued to smile even as she drifted off to sleep.

Malik was there. He was on top of her taking her on that magnificent journey to bliss once more. She rode the sensations, loving the feel of him inside her, the tightness of her body gripping him.

He called her name, said it like she was the only woman in the world for him, over and over and over again.

"I love you," she whispered. "I don't know how it happened but I love you. I truly do." The words tumbled from her mouth as her nails dug into his shoulder.

When he stilled over her, both of them reaching their climax simultaneously, Belinda wanted to weep with joy.

In the blink of an eye, she wanted to run and hide from sheer embarrassment.

The scene had shifted and she was wearing a wedding dress wrapped tightly around her slim body, veil diminishing her vision only slightly. She looked to her right and there were her parents sitting on the front pew of the church they sometimes attended. Daisy was dressed in cream-colored silk, her father looking stately in a black tuxedo, both wearing smiles that could light up the entire room. Beside her mother were her grandparents. Unlike her grandfather, her grandmother wore a slight frown.

The people in the opposite pew Belinda did not know. But at the sight of them her heart began to pound.

She hurriedly looked to her left, or rather to the man standing in front of her, at the altar of the church dressed in a tuxedo.

Patrick Masterson frowned down at her, his round face and developing second chin marred with anger or disgust, she wasn't quite sure.

"I don't love you," he said, his voice in that sickeningly high pitch of his. "I could never love a woman like you!"

Behind her Belinda heard the snickers, then the full-blown laughter of every person who sat in that church. When she looked out into the audience her grandmother was shaking her head, and her parents crying.

She'd let them down. She'd let all of them down and made a spectacle of herself, of her family.

And when she turned to run away because the weight

against her chest was bearing down so hard she could barely breathe, someone grabbed her arm.

It was Dina English and she was smiling smugly.

Belinda turned again to a maddening screech to see Carter, Shari and even Malik dripping with the red velvet cake batter she'd been using to bake those five hundred cupcakes. The room spun around her and all Belinda could hear was crying from her parents, the screeching of defeat from Shari, Patrick's taunting laugh all blending together until her eardrums burned.

And when Belinda awoke it was to sweat dripping from her forehead and a pounding in her chest. Her eyes were blurred and her mind still tried to decipher dream from reality.

She wanted to fall back onto her pillow face-first and cry from the agony of anxiety. For the past few months she'd been reading books on dealing with stress. Going to a therapist was out of the question, since it would be more than embarrassing for the family to see that one of them was cracking up.

But instead of giving in, Belinda walked into the bathroom and turned on the shower. While it ran for a few minutes she practiced her breathing. In and out, steady and slow. At the same time she cleared her mind. Patrick wasn't here. She wasn't getting married. Her grandmother didn't look disappointed. It was all a dream.

Or a nightmare.

Morning had always been Malik's favorite time of day. He was so much more productive before the sun rose. That was why he'd arrived at the gym just a little after four this morning. He'd had a restless night and was filled with pent-up energy—or unleashed passion, whichever one sounded best.

Ever since his accident and the grueling year of physical therapy that had followed, swimming had become his second-favorite sport. So after his time on the treadmill and the thirty strenuous minutes of weight lifting, he finally submerged his body into the cool water of the gym's Olympic-size pool. Every lap had his shoulders burning, his legs tingling, heart racing and mind still running circles around one particular female.

She was an enigma, or at least she tried to be. He couldn't really tell. What Malik knew for certain was that none of it mattered. He wanted Belinda. And he was pretty sure she wanted him. Even if her mind wanted to fight it, her body was game for whatever he had planned. Malik wanted to plan something superspecial for the next time they made love. He wanted to show her how special she really was and not because of any of her accomplishments, but because of who she was inside.

It was with thoughts of a blissfully romantic evening that he emerged from the pool, heading to the chair where he'd thrown his towel. Only to find it missing.

The second he turned to look around for it, she was there. Up close and very personal in a black bikini that barely covered her assets. Too bad it was the wrong woman.

"Good morning, handsome," Chantelle Martin said with a smile on her face.

"Mornin'," was Malik's mildly uncomfortable response. He took the towel she held out to him.

"You look fabulous," was her next comment as she looked him up and down.

He wore swim trunks but the hungry look she was

giving him made Malik uncomfortable, as if he was naked under her perusal. He used the towel to dry off his upper body, moving slowly so the towel would also cover his bare skin. "Thanks. What are you doing here?"

"I came to see you."

"How did you know I'd be here?" Malik didn't have a routine; he liked to play things by ear for the most part. And there was a gym in his apartment building. It wasn't as good a setup as this local one, but he used it from time to time. Which begged the question of how Chantelle knew he was here.

"Don't get all uptight. I'm not a stalker. I came by your place and the doorman told me you'd gone to work out. This was the closest gym to your apartment building so I took a shot. The attendant was kind enough to grant me a guest membership when I told him I was here to see you."

It couldn't be more than six in the morning by now. "Why were you at my place so early?" he asked her. Never mind how she knew where he lived. Jarrod had been to his apartment before so he assumed the boy had told his mother, innocently, he figured.

"I had dinner last night with someone who wants to see you. I told him I'd get you the message as soon as possible." As she talked she pulled a card from the top of her bikini. How the small piece of paper had fit into that top along with her voluptuous breasts, Malik had no idea. But he kept his gaze focused on her eyebrows, figuring that was the safest place for it to be.

He took the card from her and glanced down at it. "Why would a college coach ask you to get in touch with me?"

"You are so full of questions, so early in the morning. How about we take a swim together then we can talk over breakfast?"

Belinda's words echoed in his head. He needed to tell Chantelle that whatever she was thinking would happen between them was a no go.

"No. I have to get to work. Look, Mrs. Martin," he started, figuring he'd make this as polite and concise as possible, "I enjoy coaching Jarrod. He's a good kid and I think he has a lot of potential. I think he could get into a great high school program with his basketball skills and his grades. I'll keep you abreast of whatever I can work out for him."

"And?" she asked taking a step toward him. "What does that have to do with the two of us right here and now?"

Malik wasn't used to running from women, and what he did he wouldn't exactly call running. Well, maybe in a sense it was, but he knew self-preservation was his best bet. He stepped back from her, this time putting his hands on her shoulders to keep her at arm's length. "It means that's the only thing we have to communicate about."

She arched an eyebrow—he knew because he'd still been training his gaze there.

"Oh, really? So you're telling me that you don't want any of this?"

She used a hand to signal her body, which was not necessary at all because he'd already assumed what she was referring to. He still kept his gaze on her eyebrows.

"I'm telling you that I'm not interested in any personal entanglements with you."

There, blunt and to the point and spoken in clear, concise English. It was a done deal.

She tilted her head as her arms reached up behind her and she unlatched her bikini top. "You'll change your mind."

Now he was just angry. If there was one thing Malik hated, it was a woman who didn't respect herself.

"No," he said adamantly, "I won't. And you can tell this coach to go straight to hell!" With a flick of his wrist, Malik tossed the business card in her general direction. "Cover yourself up. This is a respectable place," he told her, giving her back the towel she'd just handed him.

As he walked out of the pool area and headed to the men's locker room, he thought about the crazy world they lived in. The one where people would do just about anything for money, or fame and fortune, or all of the above.

Chapter 12

For the first time in all the years he'd worked there, Malik walked into Lillian's and felt as if he were walking into a madhouse.

When he'd arrived that morning he'd found out that Carlos had called in with car trouble, so Malik had volunteered to make the morning deliveries. It was a job he was used to doing and one he needed today because it would give him time to think about dating Belinda, killing Chantelle's ideas about them, and why Coach Rodney Sanders would want to contact him after all these years.

Unfortunately, each delivery had come with a talkative client who wanted to know about making another order, which meant Malik had spent too much time with them and was now just getting back to the bakery at almost one o'clock.

The coffee bar had a line that stretched almost to

the main cash register and display cases. Nichelle was manning the bar and moving as fast as she could since she was solo. There were also customers at the display case, where Drake was handling them with his charming smile and cordial tone. Malik headed behind the counter with the idea that he'd take over for Drake and let Drake go over to the coffee bar to help Nichelle out since he knew more about mixing those drinks than Malik did.

"They need you in the back pronto," Drake said out of earshot of the customers.

"What's going on?"

"Oven mishap. We're a couple orders behind and time is ticking."

"Are we fully staffed except for Carlos?"

Drake nodded. "Carter's got designs going. Amber's helping him out. Shari and Belinda are trying to take care of the rest."

"I'm on it," Malik said and headed to the back.

Chaos didn't quite describe this new scene.

Two of the large oven doors stood open, steam pouring out of each one, which signaled the heat was cooling down but there was definitely a problem. Instead of trying to fix them right at this moment, he went all the way to the back and disconnected the gas lines to each of them.

"Where are we?" he said, grabbing his apron and hair cap and moving to the table where Belinda stood.

"Four whole sheet cakes, eight dozen cupcakes and pastries for the Ledbetter brunch tomorrow, 285 in attendance," she rattled off without even looking up from the bowl where she mixed the glaze that would go on top of her apple streusel.

"Two sheets need icing and decorating and all the cupcakes need the same," Shari added from the other table, where she mixed more cake batter.

"Done!" was all Malik said.

Carter and Amber were on the other side of the kitchen where they were meticulously cutting and layering, pinching and slicing and everything else that came with artisan cake designs.

"I'm gonna need help with two wedding deliveries in about an hour."

Malik nodded. "Gotcha." He was layering the first sheet cake with its buttercream base. He'd just read the order sheet that had been taped on the table beside the cake. It was a girl's sweet sixteen that already had a fondant-covered number sixteen and a sugar-encrusted tiara made to top it. He would do the final assembly and have it ready for pickup in less than thirty minutes.

Then he would help Carter with the deliveries and return here to do whatever else was needed. Because this was not only his job, it was the career he'd chosen. After the one he'd dreamed of had collapsed.

"Grandma's cooking dinner tonight. She wants us all to come over," Drake said at twenty minutes after seven when they were together in the kitchen cleaning up.

The crowd had stayed past closing, until 6:53 p.m., when Carter had come from the back and locked the front door. He instructed Nichelle to only let customers out, not to invite any more in. By seven-fifteen the bakery was finally empty and Drake had taken in all the cash from both registers and sat at the kitchen counter and began the final count for the night. The others moved around, washing dishes, putting trays and pots away, storing batter and wrapping pastries for tomorrow's early morning delivery. The one which Malik volunteered to make because they didn't want to chance Carlos still having car trouble.

"I'm exhausted," Shari was the first to admit. "And I still have to leave here and pick up Andre. I don't know if I'm going to make it."

"I think Grandma wants to talk about the competition again," Drake told them.

"I have a date," Carter said as he meticulously cleaned his tools and placed them into the cloth-lined box he kept them in.

"Come on," Belinda interjected. "I'm sure there's something all of us would like to be doing other than taking that forty-five-minute drive to the estate to have dinner and talk more about work. But this is what we do and the competition is important."

Malik heard her words and he also heard the strain in her voice as she said them. Of course, he was probably the only one to hear that since the rest of her family were simply used to her being the bucket of ice water splashing over their ideas.

"That's a long drive, Belinda. And I do have a child. I know all you have to do is worry about you, but unfortunately I can't think like that."

"Andre can sleep at Grandma's until we're finished. It's not like you'll have to change his nightly routine that much," Belinda countered.

"Spoken like a woman with no kids," Shari grumbled.

Belinda's head shot up at that remark. Her gaze quickly found Malik's then just as quickly she looked away, focusing on wrapping all the ingredients to be added as finishing touches to the pastries tomorrow. The streusels and the pies were done, fillings for the Danish would be applied in the morning, as well as all the croissants she would come in early to bake. That was part of the reason Malik had volunteered to do the morning delivery. It gave him a reason to be here to help her without having to hear her tell him she didn't need him.

"Well, I'm going," she snapped finally.

"We didn't doubt that for one minute," Carter said with a shake of his head.

"All of us should go," Malik added in an attempt to take the mounting pressure off Belinda. "If it's about the competition, we should all be there. Remember Ms. Lillian said we're in this together, as a team. How's it going to look if only part of the team shows up at a strategizing meeting?"

"That's not what it's going to be and you know it," Carter said. "If Grandma really wanted to talk business she would have called a meeting like she normally does. If she's been cooking all day, that means she wants some family time, which I can pass on when there's a lady like Cindy Carmichael waiting for me."

"*The* Cindy Carmichael?" Drake asked. He'd looked up from counting the money to see if Carter were serious.

Carter's answer was a wiggle of his eyebrows and a nod of his head.

"Yeah, maybe he should be allowed a pass on this one," Drake added.

"He should be allowed a pass so he can go get laid?" Belinda asked with disgust.

Carter chuckled. "You know, it's something you

should probably look into doing sometime this century, Belinda. It could relieve a lot of that stress you're carrying."

Malik clenched his teeth as Belinda's gaze quickly shifted to his.

"Priorities, Carter. We're talking about priorities here," Malik told his longtime friend.

Carter gave him a look of shock, then dismal pity.

After a few awkward seconds Carter sighed. "Whatever you say, man. But I'm not staying long."

"I'm not driving, so who's picking me up?" Shari asked, slamming pots into a bottom cabinet.

Her mood hadn't been the sunniest today. Malik noticed, so he knew the others did, as well. Wisely, none of them commented. They merely looked at each other, silently trying to decide who would volunteer to drive her and her mood to dinner tonight.

"Are you okay?" Malik asked Belinda the moment she arrived at her grandmother's house.

It was a lovely estate in Glenville Heights, the gorgeously scenic neighborhood running alongside Lake Michigan with tree-lined streets and palatial homes. Each time she'd driven through the black wrought iron gates along the curving driveway outlined with lush green grass and huge evergreen trees, she felt overwhelmed with pride. Her grandmother had come from an urban Chicago neighborhood. She'd raised Belinda's uncle Dwight in a modest two-bedroom apartment, the upper half of a duplex, near downtown Chicago so she would be close to work. When she'd met her second husband, they'd moved into a town house near Midway Airport. By the time Belinda had been born, the

entire family was living on this estate, now affection-
ately called Drayson Drive.

In addition to the five-bedroom, three-bath main
house, there were two other smaller homes and a pool
house located on the estate. Before her parents had
moved into their own house, they'd occupied one of
the smaller ones on the property. Now, only Lillian
and Henry lived on Drayson Drive. All this space and
only the two of them; that thought made Belinda sad.

Not only did she come into the house with a melan-
choly feeling, she was bone tired from the exertion of
the day's work and she was sleepy. Last night's nightmare had robbed her of rest and, unfortunately, of the
peace of mind she'd been striving for.

And now Malik was in her face.

She just simply wasn't in the mood.

"I'm fine," she said tightly.

"You look a little stressed."

She frowned. "Gee, thanks."

Pushing past him, she tried to move out of the foyer.
Her grandmother would be in the kitchen. When Lillian
cooked dinner, that's where she stayed until her guests
were seated and the blessing was about to be said.

But Malik grabbed her by the arm. "Hold on a second. You're not fine. I can tell."

"That's right, because you can read my thoughts.
You can tell what I'm feeling, what I'm thinking. You
just know everything!"

She shouted the last sentence, even though it wasn't
her intention. Closing her eyes she tried for calm. "I
apologize."

Malik still held her arm, his fingers tracing a slow
line upward. "It's okay. I'm just a little worried about

you, that's all. And I know tonight is going to be even more stressful. So I want you to know I'm here, you can lean on me."

That would be easy, she thought, looking into his warm brown eyes. He was so handsome and so enticing. Leaning on him and letting him take over would be so easy. But would it be right? This was her life, her family, her battle. It just wasn't fair to dump it all in Malik's lap.

"I'll be fine. Thank you," she said, then moved away from him before he could reach for her again. Before he could try to change her mind.

Chapter 13

"I saw Dina English's name on the guest list for the fund-raiser on Saturday," Daisy said as they all sat at the massive dining room table enjoying coffee and Lillian's lemon tart for dessert.

Belinda nearly jumped as Shari's fork clattered against her plate. "Did you invite her, Aunt Daisy?" Shari asked.

"No, dear. I would never do that," was Daisy's slow reply. "But this is a fund-raiser. Anyone who donates can purchase tickets. I cannot turn her away."

"She's right," Uncle Dwight replied. "Her donation is as good as anyone else's."

"It doesn't matter if she attends the fund-raiser," Monica said, reaching out a hand to touch her sister's. "We're still going to win the competition."

Shari didn't look like she'd heard a word Monica

said. Her gaze was focused down at the table, her lips drawn in a tight line.

"It's going to be hard to win if we can't stay focused on the competition instead of an old family feud," Belinda said. All eyes fell to her—some accusatory, some reflecting the pity they wanted her to give to Shari and another with perplexity—but she didn't cringe.

This personal vendetta Shari had against Dina could cost them the competition. That was a fact. Ignoring it to placate Shari wasn't the answer. No matter how sorry she felt for her cousin and the betrayal that seemed to haunt her more than it did any of the rest of the family.

"I'll be focused, Belinda. You don't have to worry about the first thing you've ever lost coming at my hand," Shari retorted.

Now she was angry with Belinda. But Belinda didn't care. She'd rather Shari be angry with her, angry enough to want to prove her point, just as she had when they'd been growing up. Shari had always felt inferior to the other Drayson cousins—why, Belinda had no idea. But it had been her mother who'd tried to explain the dynamic of the cousins' competition. One day one of them would run Lillian's. Until the time that one was selected, they were all on what seemed like an endless audition. Shari seemed to take that to heart.

"It's not about a win for me, Shari. This is for the family," Belinda told her.

"She's right," Carter chimed in. "We have to focus on each other, on our team. Not on Dina English."

"Even though we plan to kick her butt thoroughly," Drake added.

Malik only nodded at those words, his eyes still focused on her. Belinda wished he'd stop staring at her like that. As if he were looking straight through to her soul, peeling away each layer of the wall she'd built around herself. He wanted things from her she knew she couldn't give, probably didn't have to give. And at some point she'd have to tell him that was futile. But not until after the fund-raiser, since he'd agreed to be her date.

"Let's stop all this shop talk. This family is about more than the bakery," Grandpa interjected.

The entire room went quiet as he took Grandma's hand in his.

"We're a family and we all love each other. There's no need to bite off each other's heads, or place blame that hasn't been earned. And I don't want any of you going into this contest thinking of what it can do for you personally," he continued.

"That's right," Lillian said, nodding her head. "If the bakery wins, that's wonderful for the whole bakery. Not just for Carter or for Shari. It's for everyone."

Belinda didn't reply because she didn't believe that was true. Everybody had their own agenda. She knew that as surely as she knew her own name. Carter wanted more recognition for his work, Drake wanted more notoriety for the bakery and his blog, and Shari, of course, wanted revenge. As for Belinda, she wasn't sure what she wanted.

With that her gaze fell right to Malik, who was still looking at her. And then for whatever reason she looked toward her mother, who was also staring at her, with a look of displeasure. Totally uncomfortable now, Belinda excused herself from the table.

She was upset. Malik could tell by the stiffness of her shoulders and her furrowed brow. When she left the table, he did the same, following her into the den, where she'd opened the doors to the deck and now stood at the railing looking out.

There was a great view here of more plush trees and land, right out onto Lake Michigan with its eerie dark shimmer in the dimness of night. A light breeze had picked up and Belinda folded her arms across her chest.

"Tired of the scene already?" he asked, stepping out into the night with her.

"Just tired period," she told him.

He sighed, coming to stand right beside her. "I hear you on that one. I'm beat."

"Then why'd you volunteer to run that delivery in the morning? Carlos will probably show up. It's his job anyway."

"I want to make sure it gets out and on time. If he's having car trouble, there's no telling how long it'll take to be fixed, or if he can even fix it. I didn't hear from him any more today."

"He should still find a way to work. That's his responsibility."

"It is. But sometimes circumstances get in the way. I'm sure Carlos will do whatever he can to get there."

"He doesn't have to now since you volunteered to do the delivery. You've given him a pass to come in as late as he wants."

Malik nodded and let her words sink it. She wasn't yelling, in fact she sounded as tired as she'd told him she was. And yet, her words were just as callous and coldhearted.

"Carlos is a good worker."

"He's a delivery guy. It doesn't take a rocket scientist to do his job and we can just as easily find another one. A more dependable one."

Malik hadn't thought she could offend him. He'd been wrong. "I was a delivery guy, remember?"

She looked at him then, the breeze sweeping wisps of hair across her face. "You worked your way up."

"As can Carlos."

"Not if he keeps pulling stunts like this. Look, I know what it takes to run a successful bakery. I need people that I can depend on to be there and to do their jobs."

"*You* need?" Malik asked with an irritated chuckle. "You don't run Lillian's, Belinda. Not yet anyway."

She waited a beat and shrugged.

"Listen, why don't I come over to your place tonight. We can leave here and I'll follow you home."

She turned to face him then. "I don't need another bath and I can fix my own glass of wine," she told him.

A slap to his face wouldn't have been more painful. Unfortunately, Malik wasn't at all surprised. This was the Belinda he'd known for years, the one who knew exactly where to hit and how hard when she needed to. The one who had defensive mechanisms down to a science. He'd told himself when he decided to pursue her that he was ready for any- and everything she dished out. For a second he wondered how true that was.

"Look, I'm just offering for us to spend some time unwinding together. If you don't want a bath that's fine. I can even pass on the wine. I just didn't want to be alone tonight. I thought you might be feeling the same way."

His cell phone rang just as he finished that sentence. He reached for it and ran his finger along the screen to see who was calling. He had no idea that Belinda had leaned in for a closer look herself.

"Well, isn't that right on time," she said. "You can spend the evening with Mrs. Martin," was her final retort before she left him on the deck alone.

With a low curse Malik blocked the call. He could have gone after Belinda, but decided not to. She needed her space and so did he. She was sounding off at him like he'd done something to her, and he wasn't sure how long he was willing to be her punching bag. Last night she'd been pliable in his arms, generous in her kisses and her smiles. Why today had been totally different, he wasn't sure. But there was only so much he was willing to take from her.

"Tsk, tsk, tsk. Trouble in paradise?"

At the sound of Carter's voice Malik turned toward him even though Carter may have been the last person he wanted to talk to at this moment. "Don't go there," Malik warned.

Carter only laughed. He had a drink in one hand, most likely wine because Ms. Lillian didn't allow anything stronger in her house.

"Do you want to hear it now or do you want me to wait a little later to say it?"

"You can just keep your mouth shut. That might work," Malik replied.

"Not a chance in hell." Carter laughed again. When he sobered, he stood by Malik and tried not to smile, or at least not to smile as hard. "I told you so."

"Carter—"

Carter was holding up his free hand to cut off Malik. "Don't steal my joy because you're in a funk. I told you to stay away from Belinda. To let her live in that cold shell she'd created for herself. But no, you had to go with your body instead of your head. Or is it that you were following the lead of the wrong head?"

"Not funny," Malik chided. "And it's not what you think."

"Isn't it? Didn't my dear sweet cousin just give you the ice pick to the heart and basically tell you to go find another date for tonight?"

"I don't have a date for tonight."

"If you call back whoever that was on your phone, you would," Carter said, nodding toward the cell phone Malik still held in his hand.

He shook his head. "Not a chance. That woman is as crazy as they come."

"You must like them that way."

"I vaguely remember telling to you shut up," Malik replied with a frown, taking a seat in one of the chairs.

Carter followed suit. "I don't listen to you any more than Belinda does."

"Belinda doesn't listen to anyone but Belinda."

"No news there," Carter added. "Listen, why don't you consider coming to New York with me? I'm sure I can get you as sweet a deal as Robinson's offering me."

Malik was shaking his head before Carter could even finish his words. New York was too far away from Chicago, too far away from Belinda—the woman who he wasn't quite ready to give up on.

"No, thank you. I think I've decided that my place is here. With her," he ended with a sigh. "There's something else bothering her. Something happened. I just need to figure out what."

Carter was not amused and didn't sound like he believed what Malik was saying. "Don't waste your time, man. She's not going to change."

"I'm not asking her to change."

Carter looked surprised. "Then what are you asking of her? What is it that you want from Belinda, Malik?"

For a few moments Malik was quiet. He'd thought about this many nights, and last night he had thought of nothing else. If admitting it to Carter would solidify the fact in his mind, reassure him that he was on the right path, so be it.

"I want to marry her, to take care of her."

Carter didn't say a word. Even though Malik didn't expect him to. Actually, he half expected his arrogant friend to laugh once more. Instead Carter sat up in his chair and stared at him.

"You're serious, aren't you?" he asked.

Malik nodded. "I am. Whether or not that's the smartest thing I've ever said I don't know. But it's the truth."

"You're in love with Belinda. That's what you're saying because you wouldn't say the *m* word unless you were seriously in love."

"For years I was afraid I was in love with her. But it was just a thought. Now I know for sure. I'm in love with her."

"Then you're in more trouble than I thought," Carter quipped, then sighed and took another sip of his drink.

"You're absolutely right about that," Drake said as he, too, walked out onto the deck.

Malik hadn't called her or tried to talk to her alone for the rest of the week. Belinda couldn't blame him. She'd been a bitch the other day and she'd left him standing on that deck with his phone and that simple woman calling. She should have stayed and answered the call herself. But that wasn't something that she did. Mrs. Martin was Malik's responsibility, not hers.

And the phone call hadn't given her any right to be as obnoxious as she'd been with him. Thinking about it retrospectively was a lot easier and a lot more troubling to Belinda than it had been that day. This was not the change in life she was looking for. The dream had caused her to revert to the old her, to fall into the slump of feeling guilty about what she hadn't done, or had no control over in the first place. It was silly and she wondered now if it had cost her a date to the fund-raiser.

Not that the no-date status would stop her from going. Her mother had already called her three times today to stress the importance of her being there. Staying home was not an option. And yet it was still a very attractive thought.

When the doorbell rang, Belinda thought it was the men from the garage who she'd paid to wash and detail her car. She'd just stepped out of the shower and pulled her robe over her shoulders. Belting it tightly, she headed to the door and was beyond shocked to see her grandmother standing on the other side.

"Grandma! Hi," she said. "Come on in."

"I see I've surprised you with a visit," Lillian said, coming into the apartment.

"Let me put your purse over here," Belinda said immediately.

"I'll keep it with me," Lillian countered and continued walking without turning back.

"Sure. Have a seat," she said, rubbing her hands together then willing herself to let them drop to her side.

As much as Belinda loved her grandmother, being around her tended to make her nervous. Belinda always felt like she might be in trouble for something or that maybe she'd disappointed her grandmother somehow. And now that Lillian was here in her apartment and they were alone, she was really struggling for calm.

"So what brings you here?" she asked finally, sitting on the edge of the couch a distance away from her grandmother.

Lillian slid over closer and reached for Belinda's hands. She wanted to stuff them into her pocket but knew that would be rude. With a deep breath Belinda extended her hands.

"Relax, Belinda. It's nothing bad. You're sitting here about to hyperventilate because you can't figure out why I'm here in your personal space."

Belinda didn't want to admit that was true. "I'm just shocked, that's all."

"I know. I wanted the element of surprise," Lillian said with a chuckle.

Her heavily gray streaked hair was pulled back with two combs on each side and left hanging in heavy curls to her ears. She wore slacks and a blouse, her diamond wedding ring and a simple pearl necklace. She was elegant and classic and she smelled like lilacs, as she always had. That scent was what really calmed Belinda.

"It's silly, I know. I just get so worked up," she admitted.

"You've always been worked up, child. I told your mother years ago you were going to worry yourself to death." Lillian gave a little chuckle and patted her hand.

"I'm trying to be better," Belinda said without

thought. As soon as the words were out she wished she could snatch them back.

Lillian's eyes immediately widened like Belinda had just spoken the magic words.

"Who says you need to be better?" Lillian asked.

Belinda shook her head. "It's nothing. I shouldn't have said that. Tell me why you're here," she continued, trying to smile and stop the rapid beating of her heart at the same time.

But Lillian shook her head. "No. You tell me why you need to be better. Open your mouth and talk to me, Belinda."

She couldn't. And yet she could. Belinda knew, had always known, that she could talk to her grandmother about anything. She'd never done so because it would be admitting her failures, and the last thing she wanted was for her grandmother to believe she'd failed.

"Just thinking that since I'm getting older I should probably get better," she said with a shrug.

"Poor child," Lillian said sadly. "Good, better, best— those words have always been first in your vocabulary. If that's what you're looking to change then I agree wholeheartedly. You need to focus on just being you and doing what's good, better and best for you, Belinda."

Tears stung her eyes as she listened to her grandmother's words. "I don't know what you mean."

"Come now, you're the smartest girl I've ever met. Too smart for your own good, I suspect." Lillian continued to rub Belinda's hand. "You know what changes you want to make, what changes you think will work, but you're afraid to do it. Why is that? What are you afraid of?"

Nobody had ever asked Belinda that question before.

Maybe because she'd never acted like she was afraid of anything. Whatever the task she'd stepped up to the plate and gotten it done. There'd never been any doubt, any hesitation. Until now.

"I'm afraid that change might not be best. What if I'm wrong? What if it doesn't work?"

"And what if it does?"

She shook her head. "But it didn't. I tried to open myself up to a man, to be with someone who was so different from the kind of man I usually dated, and it backfired. He hasn't even called me all week."

"Stop it. You just stop it. This is not you. You are a much stronger woman than this. If you decided to do something and I mean really decided, you and I both know you would do it. Now, if you're talking about Malik, well, I don't think that boy has gone far. He's been watching you for so long I doubt he knows what another woman looks like."

"What? Did you say Malik? How did you know?" Belinda hadn't told anyone but Shari and she doubted her cousin had run back and told their grandmother they were dating, or whatever it was they were doing.

"I have eyes, Belinda. I can still see when a man wants a woman and when a woman is taking her own sweet time in figuring out if she wants him back. The other night when you all were at the house I could see it. You two dancing around each other like you had this big secret. Him wanting to reach out to you and you backing off. I wondered why you weren't just stepping up to the plate and grabbing that fine man in your arms, like you normally do with something you want. But now I see why. You're afraid."

"I'm not afraid of Malik."

"No, baby, you're afraid of what Malik makes you feel. You're afraid that, if you reach for him, he'll go away and you will have failed. You don't like to fail."

"No. I don't," she admitted.

"So in this instance you'd rather not try."

No, she'd rather not talk about this anymore. "I really should get dressed for the fund-raiser."

"You don't want to go so why don't you stay home?"

"My mother would have a fit if I didn't show up."

Lillian waved a hand. "Daisy would survive. She's always been a bossy one. But once you stand your ground, she'll stop pushing."

Belinda knew her grandmother was right. She'd known this all along. The only thing stopping her from moving forward was herself. And after her grandmother had hugged and kissed her and promised to stop by more frequently so they could talk openly, she'd gone into her bedroom to get dressed.

She slipped on the mint-green silk A-line gown she'd ordered on Monday and prayed it would arrive by Friday. It had arrived and it fit perfectly, thank the heavens. She'd already applied her makeup and had just retrieved her shoes when the doorbell rang again. Okay, this definitely had to be the car detailers.

Belinda hurriedly pulled open the door. Then her mouth opened, closed and opened again as she tried to figure out what to say.

"Hello, Malik." Simple and friendly was how the response sounded.

"You look astounding," was his reply, and all Belinda could do was smile.

The worry about why he hadn't called her, the fear

that he wouldn't want her if she wanted him, all of it sort of melted away as he continued to gaze at her.

"I'm not wearing any shoes," she said and realized too late how silly that sounded.

With the same smile that never failed to send her heart rate soaring, he stepped into the apartment, lifting her hand that held the shoes. "The shoes are nice, too."

She pulled her hand back slowly as he closed the door. Turning to move into the living room, she leaned on the side of the couch to slip on her shoes, then she brushed down the front of her dress, nervous energy pinging around inside her.

"I didn't think you were coming."

He nodded. "Because we haven't really seen each other in the last few days."

Belinda did something she tried not to do too often because of her mother's constant warnings about posture and decorum. She shrugged. "I just thought…" Her voice trailed off as he lifted her chin with his finger.

"You thought I was angry at the way you acted the other night at your grandmother's."

She must be as transparent as cellophane, Belinda thought. First her grandmother and now Malik. How was it possible that everyone around her had a bead on what she was feeling or thinking, but her?

"I was out of line."

Malik nodded. "You were. But I suspect there was a reason."

She shook her head. "None that bears mentioning. Just my atychiphobia kicking in," she said blithely. "Oh, that's the fear of—"

"It's the fear of failure, I know," he responded for her.

"I know a little bit about failing, Belinda. You're not the only one who wanted to be perfect at something."

She figured he was talking about his basketball career but wasn't sure if he wanted to continue talking about it. "You were injured. It wasn't your fault that you couldn't play anymore."

"I know that. Just like I know you do not have atychiphobia. You're too intelligent and too successful to really possess that fear. This thing between us is new and it's unchartered territory for you, so it's understandable that you don't know how to dominate the situation just yet."

She tilted her head to look up at him closely. There was definitely something about this man that drew her to him. It had been a slow draw, one she suspected had been going on way longer than the time she'd decided to make a change in her life. He'd been around for years now and not until recently had she looked at him in this way. She wondered why, then decided not to give it any more thought. For whatever reason, they were standing here in her living room at this moment, together. That was all that mattered.

"And how long are you going to be this patient with me, Malik? Why do you put up with me when you know all my faults?"

"Because what I know with even more clarity, and what matters even more to me than your faults, is that I'm in love with you."

Okay, that knocked a few cubes out of her confidence cup. Belinda never would have expected those words from him. Yet here they were, lingering in the air like a fine mist, one that settled over her and filled her chest so that she now felt the urge to cough or cry or maybe both.

"I don't know what to say," was her final response.

Malik chuckled. "That's a first. Belinda Drayson-Jones at a loss for words. I must be better than I thought."

That made her smile. Malik made her smile and he made her feel comfortable and cherished, not worshiped or with any type of expectancy. No, when she was with him, she just felt happy. And that was enough.

Chapter 14

The Ivy Room was located just two blocks from the Magnificent Mile and was the embodiment of history and artistic elegance. It had been the venue for everything from couture fashion shows to live band performances. Tonight, however, this beautiful structure, with its ivy-covered walls and ballroom windows that boasted picturesque views, was the locale for Daisy Drayson-Jones's event of the season.

Her mother had rented out the courtyard and the lower level for this high-powered moneymaking event because for Daisy there was no limit to success. It shocked Belinda that with all Lillian's coaching and grooming of her, Daisy had never done very much with her own life, until now.

The sun had just begun to set and the courtyard was lit with twinkle lights and candles on the highboy tables. Lilies in all their pristine beauty flanked the podiums and occupied large crystal vase arrangements. A quartet dressed impeccably in black tuxedoes played music that reminded Belinda of the cotillions she'd attended as a young girl. People of all races moved about with glasses of champagne in their hands, talked in hushed whispers, probably about how much they planned to give or not give. It was the perfect event, the perfect evening…for her mother.

That thought hit her as she and Malik made their way inside and she stopped.

"Are you all right?" he asked.

Belinda looked up at him and wondered what the hell had taken her so long. She almost laughed as the memory surfaced of her and Malik on the floor at the roller-skating rink, holding on to each other for dear life, praying they wouldn't end up sprawled on the floor.

"I'm just fine," she replied, squaring her shoulders once more. "I don't really feel like being here. Do you mind if I just find my mother and speak to her, then we can leave?"

"If that's what you want to do," he said, lacing her arm through his. "I'll take you wherever you want to go."

"Thank you, Malik." She doubted he had any idea what she was really thanking him for.

Malik talked to a few people he knew that were surprised to see him here. After his stint with the NBA he'd made a point to stay out of the limelight. Sure, he could have continued with more rehab and tried to get back on another team, but he hadn't. He could have applied for a coaching job or taken a scout position. He hadn't done that, either. Instead, he'd started over in a career no one would ever guess he'd be interested in. He'd re-invented himself and now he liked the person he was. Most of the time.

"Well, well, well. If I'd known you were going to be here tonight, I wouldn't have spent that evening wining and dining Mrs. Martin."

Malik turned from the bar, where he'd been standing watching the guests mill about. He'd already had a glass of champagne and wanted something by way of a beer instead. He and the bartender were conversing about why there was none available at this event.

"Hello, Rodney," Malik said, speaking cordially to his former college coach.

"You're a hard person to catch up with, Malik," Rodney said as he accepted a glass of champagne from the bartender.

It seemed that sparkling water and lemonade were the only beverages on tap for the evening. Which for Malik really sucked. He looked over at the man he used to worship, the one he'd spent more time with than any other man in his life and tried to smile.

"Not really," he told him. "I'm listed in the phone book."

Rodney chuckled and Malik noticed the lines around his eyes. It was also the first time he noticed the graying at Rodney's temples and peppered throughout his rough-cut goatee.

"Guess we've just been missing each other then," Rodney said, taking a sip from his glass.

"I guess so. But using Chantelle Martin to get to me is a no go. I don't know what she may have told you, but we're not personally involved." Malik had an idea of what Chantelle had told him their involvement was, and he wanted to be sure to clear the air.

"She didn't talk all that much when we spent the evening together."

He was definitely not surprised to hear that. Not on the part of Chantelle, or Rodney for that matter.

"Doesn't matter," Rodney continued. "The past is the past, Malik. I've always told you that."

"You told me a lot of stuff."

"And you were a good listener."

"Too bad you weren't a good example of practicing what you preach."

"That's not fair. Everything I taught you, everything about our relationship, was on the up-and-up."

Malik had to laugh at that. At the absurdity of what had just been said to him.

"What about your relationship with my mother? Was that on the up-and-up, too? Was sleeping with the mother of your star player a part of the grand plan to make Malik Anthony the number-one draft pick into the NBA?"

Rodney finished his champagne. "You don't know what you're talking about."

"I don't know that you and my mother were having an affair the entire time I played ball for you? Or maybe I don't know that this is how it works in the real world—if parents want their kids to play professional ball they have to learn to do whatever it takes. Isn't that what you told my mother when she tried to break it off? That night as I lay in my hospital bed with my knee torn to shreds, didn't you tell her to meet you in your hotel room and you'd see what you could do about getting me healed and onto another team?"

"Slow down, son. Just slow down. You're going so deep into the past now. Things have changed since then. People change."

Malik turned quickly but remembered where he was. "You don't change. You were a conniving sonof-abitch then and you're still one now. Do I need to ask Mrs. Martin how your dinner date ended? What did you promise to do for Jarrod so she'd sleep with you?"

"Malik?"

He whirled around fast to see Belinda standing behind him, a quizzical look on her beautiful face.

"Is everything all right?"

She stepped to him then, her hand going to his arm. Then as if she just noticed the man beside him she said, "Hello."

"Good evening, ma'am. I'm Rodney Sanders, coach—"

Malik stepped between them, shielding Belinda from Rodney. "You're nobody. You got that? You are nobody to me so stay the hell out of my life!"

When he turned again it was to grab Belinda by the arm and stalk off.

He had no idea how long they sat on that little cement bench looking at the stars, hearing the music playing in the background, Belinda's hand rubbing along his back. She hadn't said a word since he'd pulled her away, only sat quietly while he sorted through the myriad emotions attacking his body.

Anger didn't quite describe what he was feeling at the moment. Rage, maybe? Hurt, definitely. And that was most likely what continued to fuel the rage. He'd tried for so long not to think about this, not to have to deal with this part of his past. And for years it had worked. Obviously his vacation from the hell of his life was abruptly over.

"I didn't grow up like you did, Belinda. My parents weren't in love with each other and we didn't take family vacations." He took a deep breath, kept his elbows planted firmly on his knees and didn't dare turn back to look at her.

"My father left before I was born. I don't even know him. My mother worked two jobs to make sure I had clean clothes and food and that I went to school. When I started playing basketball at the rec center after school, I guess she got ideas. She married this guy that had a little bit of money but didn't give a crap about raising another man's kid, and we moved across town. It was a nice neighborhood with nice kids, even if they were all white. I didn't really fit in, but I could play ball. So I made the high school team and I hung out with all the cool kids. This guy started hanging around after my games, watching me. I knew about scouts and all that from my mother. She was the first one to tell me I'd play for the NBA one day. I believed her because a mother wouldn't lie to her child. She believed I could do it, so I did, too."

Belinda's hand continued to rub his back, a constant source of warmth that was succeeding in calming him down a bit.

"That guy that kept hanging around, showed up at my house for dinner one night. Then we took a plane to meet him at his school and stayed in a lavish hotel for the weekend. He had a lot of meetings with my mother that weekend." Malik shook his head. "A lot of damn meetings without me. But I was too starstruck to see why." He inhaled deeply, exhaled slowly.

"I ended up playing for him in college. He taught me everything about the game, about how to play with the pros and how to make it in the NBA. He was my mentor. No, he was more than that. He was the closest thing I'd ever had to a father."

"The guy at the bar?" she asked.

Malik nodded. "Coach Rodney Sanders. Legendary for the amount of students he'd sent to the NBA, the amount of basketball phenoms he'd discovered. And for the amount of women he'd used to build his legend."

"I don't understand."

She wouldn't, he thought dismally. Belinda would not understand how someone could use someone else to get ahead, because that's not the world she came from. She would, however, understand the hunger that had burned like an inferno in the gut of a young boy who wanted to make his mother proud. But those types of blemishes weren't in her perfect and pristine life. And he didn't begrudge her for that.

"I played for seven months in the NBA. Got a sweet car, a fat check and more attention than I've ever had in my life. Then in one game I was knocked to the floor by a seasoned veteran. Through the roar of the crowd, I heard the muscles in my leg stretch and moan in agony. The next few days were a blur. All I kept hearing was that I'd torn my ACL and I would probably never play professionally again. For days that was all I heard, then one day I heard something else. It was Coach Sanders talking to my mother, who was angry with him for not protecting me better. He told her that he could work something out for me if she resumed their relationship."

"Oh, Malik," Belinda sighed, laying her head on his shoulder. "I'm so sorry."

Malik shook his head. "He'd been sleeping with my mother the entire time. It was her payment for him coaching me, grooming me. Everything he'd said and done for me was a lie, because she was a married woman sleeping with his trifling ass!"

It sounded one-sided, Malik knew. His mother had known exactly what she was doing and had used him as an excuse. Malik's anger had not been spared on either of them. But at the end of the day, Jocelyn Kincaid was his mother. She was the woman who'd worked at Burger King at night and at the local supermarket during the day to keep a roof over his head. She'd sometimes gone without pretty dresses and shoes, so that he could get new basketball shoes or a new uniform for the team. There was nothing Jocelyn wouldn't do for her only son, including betray her husband.

As for the coach, Malik hated the sight of him, hated the air the man breathed. He'd already received letters from Sanders and voice mails to his home phone, which he rarely ever answered. He couldn't believe the gall of the man to come here and actually look for him.

"Sorry, I didn't mean to dump all this on you," he said finally, sitting up and taking her hand in his.

"No. I'm glad you told me. I'm glad I could be here for you," she told him honestly.

"I walked away from the NBA and the sport of basketball for almost two years. Then I figured that wasn't really hurting anybody but myself. I had some of the signing bonus money left so I went to a financial investor and told him my idea of a nonprofit foundation. He

set up everything for me and I've been running Hoop'n
Stars ever since."

"It's a great program," she told him. "I did some re-
search and you're reaching thousands of kids nationwide."

He smiled because she'd given him this information
so matter-of-factly like they were at a business meeting
and he needed to be told how his company was faring.
"You researched me?"

"Not you," she said slowly, probably unsure of
whether or not he'd be angry about that fact. "The company, because I wanted to see what other types of things
you do and figure out if I could somehow help."

Now, that was a surprise. "You want to help with
the foundation?"

"I want to help girls like Kayla. She looked so sad
that day. Then her team won and she ran off the mat and
hugged me. I've never been hugged like that before."

She was smiling and leaning into him, and he could
see excitement brewing in her eyes.

"Anyway, I found out that her mother works all the
time and Kayla just goes to the rec around her neighborhood to keep from being home alone. I saw her at
the library the day before yesterday and she's an excellent reader. She says her grades are really good in
school, too."

"Wait a minute. You're contacting her without her
mother's permission?"

Belinda held up a hand. "I'm not stupid, Malik. I've
always contributed financially to the libraries around
the city, but last year I started going in one day a week
during the summer for the youth reading program. The

rec center brought the kids there on the same day I was there getting the schedule for this summer."

"I didn't know you read at the library."

She nudged him and smiled brightly. "See, you don't know everything about me."

"I will," he said, bringing up her hand to his lips for a kiss. "I want to know all there is to know about you so I can take care of you and—"

"Isn't this a lovely surprise?"

This must be the week for interruptions and over-heard conversations, Malik thought.

"Hello, Belinda. Your mother said I'd find you out here with your little friend."

Malik had already been eyeing this guy with re-served interest. He hadn't liked his tone from the first comment. The second one, including the reference to him being a "little friend," was about to earn him an ass kicking. Coach Sanders had already ruffled his feath-ers, so it wasn't going to take much to push him over the edge. With that in mind, Malik stood slowly and extended his hand in a gentlemanly fashion.

"Malik Anthony, and you are?"

"Patrick Masterson of Masterson Wholesale Foods."

His grip was weak as he shook Malik's hand.

"I didn't expect to see you here, Patrick," Belinda said from beside Malik.

Her entire body had gone stiff, so he knew she wasn't comfortable with this guy and he wondered why.

"I told your mother I'd be here, since she called my office a couple times to request my presence."

He had the nerve to smile at Malik when he said that. This guy was truly a character, with his expen-sive tuxedo and sparkling diamond cuff links peeking from his sleeves. A couple inches shorter than Malik, Patrick Masterson had an early receding hairline that wasn't helped by the fact that he tried to let his hair grow out. He had a thick, not muscular, build, but carried himself as though he thought that was the going preference these days.

"Then maybe you should go back out there to find her," was Belinda's retort. "We're about to leave."

With that said, she grabbed hold of Malik's hand. Malik was just about to wish the jerk a good-night when he did exactly what Malik figured he'd do.

"This is the best you could do after me? If I'd known you were this desperate to go after some washed-up basketball player I would have stayed with you no matter how stuck-up you are. Your family deserves better than this guy."

Malik felt his fingers releasing Belinda's. He heard her whisper something like, "Let's just go." But he was so beyond that point.

With one step in Patrick's direction, Malik took a swing and knocked the jackass a couple feet back, where he fell right into an ivy topiary draped in twinkle lights.

From behind he heard Belinda gasp. When he turned, it was to see her covering her mouth and Daisy Drayson-Jones making her way over to them, a small crowd following behind her.

Chapter 15

"I just cannot believe you would do this to me, Belinda. And what is he doing here anyway?" Daisy asked, flinging a hand in the direction of the doorway where Malik stood.

She and her mother were in one of the dressing rooms on the lower level of the Ivy Room. Patrick's mother and father had helped him out of the bush and the bartender sent over napkins and a bucket of ice to assuage his broken nose.

"Malik is my date for the evening," Belinda answered coolly.

"He's your date? You brought a coworker to this important function?"

"Who would you have rather I brought, Mama? The arrogant ass that called me stuck-up?"

Daisy touched a finger to her temple, lightly because it would never do to mess up her makeup. "Lower your voice. Don't you think we've managed to embarrass the family enough tonight? Or rather, I'll say your little date over there has embarrassed us enough."

"At least he was bold enough to stand up for me," she shot back.

"What kind of juvenile response is that?" Daisy asked, her perfectly arched eyebrows shooting upward.

Her mother looked stunning in the beige-and-gold-taffeta gown. Her nails were done, diamonds shimmering; in fact, everything about Daisy spoke elegance, privilege, perfection.

But she wasn't perfect. Belinda knew this for a fact. She'd let Lillian down by not becoming a baker, and she'd let her only daughter down by caring more about some crazy blown-out-of-control protocol and decorum code that most likely didn't even exist. Belinda realized in that instant that her mother had taken—no, prohibited—much more in Belinda's life than she'd actually given her. And that was not to be tolerated any longer.

"It's the kind of response I'm giving you. Malik is a good man, regardless of who his parents are or where his family lineage lies. He's a good man because he's the one I want to be with. And I wouldn't pick someone who wasn't good."

"Okay, whatever. We need to get back out there and smooth things over with the Mastersons. Patrick's threatening to file charges against Malik and sue me for not having appropriate security to screen uninvited guests at this function."

Was she serious? Belinda looked at her mother, wondering how this woman could be the daughter of Lillian Drayson. When did she become so distorted in her values and when did everyone else besides her daughter become so important?

"You go smooth things over with the Mastersons. They can go to hell for all I care." With that said, Belinda lifted her dress so she wouldn't trip as she marched across the room, heading toward Malik and the door.

"Belinda, you come right back here. I'm your mother!"

Belinda turned at that. "You are. But I'm my own woman and I'll make my own decisions from here on out."

He'd driven them to his place. Not for any specific reason but that she'd never been there before and he felt like going home. And he wanted her with him, without the distraction of her family or her things that she kept so neat and tidy, the routine of her normal life.

"This is nice," she said when she walked into the living room from the front foyer.

As far as space, her apartment was bigger, but his had more furniture, more things, which said someone actually lived here. He'd noticed that about her place—the sparse decorations, the simplistic, almost sterile, environment. It was so simple and yet so intense at the same time. And when she was there, she'd been fighting for control. Malik had seen it and had wanted to make it better.

"Have a seat," he told her.

"I want to look around first," she said. "If you don't mind?"

He shook his head and picked up the remote from the bookshelf. Malik supposed it was typical guy fashion, but he didn't really care. For him, the remote that controlled everything in this room was for convenience and served its purpose marvelously. With the flick of a button he switched on the two lamps that sat on matching end tables on either side of his black leather couch. His carpet was a deep gray, the bookshelf, entertainment center and matching tables all black. On his walls every picture was framed in the same black-and-silver frame, the pictures were black and whites of different city skylines.

"I love Paris," she said wistfully as she looked up at the picture on the wall behind the couch. "Don't you?"

"I've never been. But I liked the picture."

She nodded. "You always just buy what you like?"

"Usually. Well, after I could afford to buy what I liked, that is."

"But you're not with the NBA anymore, how can you... I mean, where..." She shook her head, refusing to finish her sentence. "Never mind. It's not important."

"Yes, it is," Malik said. He'd removed his tuxedo jacket and slipped his hands into his pockets as he leaned on the arm of the couch. "To you, it would be important how I make my living. You already know where I work and about how much I make there. What you don't know is that, as the first-round draft pick, I was paid a lot of money to sign with the NBA. Even though I couldn't fulfill my entire contract, which was three years, I still walked away with all of my signing bonus and a good portion of the remaining contract. That was courtesy of a very good agent. After I left, I told you I met with an investor."

"To start the foundation," she said, looking at him intently, like every word he said was totally being absorbed.

"That and to talk about my future. I've made some pretty good investments in the last few years. So much so that I'm very comfortable, without the salary from the bakery."

Now she looked incredulous. "Then why do you work at the bakery? I mean why do you stay there working for someone else when you could have your own bakery or anything else you wanted?"

"Maybe I like the scenery at the bakery."

She smirked. "Come on, I may be new at this relationship thing but I'm not that naive."

Malik chuckled. "You're right. Baking is peaceful to me. It's not the constant rush of running up and down the court, constant competing, constantly trying to be the best player. I can be creative and relaxed when I bake." He shrugged. "I don't know, that's just the way it worked out."

"All things happen for a purpose," she said, coming to stand closer to him.

Malik couldn't help it. If she was near, he wanted to touch her. So he did. With both hands he cupped her face.

"My grandmother says that all the time." She continued talking as her hands moved to his arms.

"I hate that he hurt you," Malik said, his thumbs caressing the softness of her cheeks. She tried to shake her head.

"I don't want to talk about him. I don't want to think about him. He's an idiot."

"And an ass and I'll bet he's rethinking saying another word to you after tonight."

She smiled and everything inside Malik warmed.

He loved her smile, how it lit up her eyes and added a glow to her skin.

"He's thinking about pressing charges," she replied.

"Let him." Malik really didn't care. To protect Belinda, he would take anything Patrick Masterson dished out, and anyone else for that matter.

"I'm sorry. This isn't how I meant for this evening to end," she told him.

"It's not how it's going to end," was his reply.

He moved in slowly, touching his lips to hers in a soft whisper. "I'm going to make long, sweet love to you tonight, Belinda."

Their lips touched again, this time his tongue brushing softly against hers. Her breath hitched, that tiny little sound that was like music to his ears.

"I'm going to let you make long, sweet love to me tonight, Malik," she whispered against his lips.

And Malik smiled.

The blindfold was cool against her face at first and the loss of sight a little unnerving. But when Malik put his lips to her ear and whispered, "Trust me, baby," Belinda's heart rate immediately calmed.

She was naked on his bed—which was a huge-ass bed for one person. His room was red. Yes, red, and it had been a shock to her the moment she had walked in and he switched on the lights. The walls were a deep, almost bloodred, the curtains sheer and black. Candles were everywhere as if this were actually some type of worship area. He'd laughed when she said that.

"The only thing I plan to worship tonight is you, sweetness."

Was it possible to orgasm just from the sound of a

man's voice? That's the question she'd asked herself when he said those words and she felt like her legs would give out beneath her.

He touched her arms, fingers moving softly over her skin before his lips landed quick, moist kisses on her neck and throat. She arched her back when he kissed her breasts, licking around each nipple so slowly she wanted to yell with impatience. He traced little circles with his fingers around her breasts, then along the skin beneath her breasts and down her torso. Everywhere he drew a circle he followed up with his tongue as if it were tracing the invisible lines.

Belinda felt each touch right down to her toes. When he turned her over she wondered what in the world he would do back there. Obviously there was no need to wonder. Malik had a plan.

His tongue moved along the line of her back, then his fingers traced there, massaging her spine until she moaned. She was startled when his lips touched her bottom, kissing along the roundness and down the backs of her thighs. When he traced a finger down the crease of her behind, she hissed. And when that finger went farther and farther until it was parting the moist folds of her vagina, she could do nothing but cry out.

He entered her from behind, his thick length pressing through the damp path prepared just for him.

Malik moaned. No, he almost cried out with the pleasure that rippled through his body so quick and intense his shoulders shook. With his hands gripping her hips he pulled her so that she came up on her knees, the top half of her still flat on the bed, and he thrust. In and out, back and forth, he sank inside her, realizing there was no other place like this, no other woman for him.

He moved slowly, excruciatingly so, but that's how he'd imagined this night ending. Sure, his knuckles were a little sore from punching that jackass at the fundraiser, but he didn't care. All of it was worth this exact moment.

Beneath him she moaned and he absorbed the sound, loving it more each time she did it. When she began circling her hips to match his thrust Malik cursed. If she kept that up, he wasn't going to be able to make this last as long as he wanted.

Switching positions he sat on the edge of the bed, pulling her on top of him, clasping her legs behind his back. He guided her slowly onto his length, let her head fall forward to rest on his chest for a moment.

"You feel exquisite," he whispered in her ear.

"I never knew it could be like this," she admitted, and reached for her blindfold, tearing it off. "I want to see you, see what you do to me," she said.

Malik couldn't argue with that. He definitely couldn't argue with the way she jutted her chest out with that last sentence, rubbing stiff nipples along the light spray of hair on his chest. She lifted her hips slightly then dropped them back down and Malik gritted his teeth.

Belinda moved on top of him like an experienced lap dancer and she was giving him the best damn performance of her life. With desire building like a volcano waiting to erupt inside of him, Malik lowered his face to her breasts, which swayed against his mouth as she moved. He pumped faster as he heard his name over and over again, louder and louder. Fear that he might hurt her scurried along his mind as he held her waist so tight, pumping so deep into her she'd arched her back and screamed. In the next instant Malik's release tore through him with ferocious strength.

It seemed hours later that he was able to move, that he caught his breath. He wrapped his arms around her, hugging her as close to him as he possibly could, burying his face in the crook of her neck.

Belinda hugged him back with the same strength, her nails lightly scraping his back.

"I am so in love with you, Belinda."

She sighed and Malik feared she was thinking about his words, wondering if he meant them or should she say them in return. He was about to pull back, to look her in the eyes and assure her that he was being completely truthful. But she held him tighter.

"Me, too, Malik. I love you, too."

Chapter 16

"You told me that night on the deck at my grandmother's to mind my business. Out of respect I did. But the next time you plan on getting my mother all riled up, I wish you'd give me a heads-up," Drake had said as he, Carter and Malik played basketball.

The three of them met on the courts whenever they were all available. An early morning call from Carter had initiated this game. Malik hadn't complained even though he'd been pretty damned comfortable with Belinda wrapped softly around him as they lay in bed sleeping in after their long night of lovemaking. But he'd recognized what this call was really for and tore himself away from the woman of his dreams to join her cousin and brother in what might be the real fight of his life.

"I took your sister to a fund-raiser that your mother forced her to attend. How was I supposed to know that fool Masterson was going to be there and wasn't going to know when to shut his ignorant mouth?" Malik asked, catching the ball Carter had tossed his way.

"I heard you broke his nose with a sucker punch," Carter added with a grin.

Malik passed the ball back to him with a forceful push. "I punched that sucker in the face for speaking out of turn to my woman. No big deal."

Drake, who wasn't as good a player as Malik or Carter, stood in front of both of them, stopping their progress by his serious stance.

"You embarrassed my mother and thus the family. Our image is everything. This competition is coming up, commercials are going to start running. TV crews will be at the bakery getting live shots. We have the book deal, the blog, we're about to be in the spotlight. Don't you two get it?" Drake implored.

"Get a grip, Drake." Carter frowned. "You're the one who doesn't get it. You and Aunt Daisy. Malik was protecting Belinda's honor. Quite chivalrous of him, I'd say. Wouldn't you protect your woman from a jerk like Masterson?"

Drake shook his head. "We're not talking about me or my woman. We're talking about Malik, a member of this team, and Belinda, who is my sister, so I don't even want to think about who she's sleeping with, and who is also a member of this team. You heard what Grandma said—we have to think like a team."

"And like a team, I'd think if I wasn't there, either one of you would have done the same thing I did," Malik retorted, already tired of Drake's irritating conversation.

To an extent, Drake was a lot like Daisy, only he didn't push Belinda's buttons. Malik thought that might be because Drake was just a little afraid of his sister.

"Of course I wouldn't let anybody disrespect my sister. I'm just irritated because I know this is going to be in the papers and I'm going to have to figure out damage control."

"I think the damage has been controlled. Masterson got his nose patched up and Malik went home with the girl. Case closed. Now can we play ball?" Carter said, tossing the ball to Drake, who barely caught it before it could slam into his face.

"Fine," Drake said tightly, tossing the ball right back to Malik with the same force. "Hurt my sister and I'll kill you."

Malik caught the ball without a problem and smiled at Drake. "Right," was his only reply before he ran past Drake to post a layup that was nothing but net.

Three days later the scene at the bakery seemed to be the same, but was drastically different. They were all working at the bakery, going about their daily business, but there was a chill in the air. One that Belinda sensed revolved around Shari.

"Is she okay?" Malik asked Belinda later that afternoon, talking about Shari.

She hadn't known what to say. For once she really didn't have an answer. "I don't know. She seems a little tense, doesn't she?"

"Everybody does if you ask me," Malik commented, looking directly at Carter. Belinda figured whatever was going on there, Malik knew about, since he and Carter were as close as brothers. She'd thought about pressing further to find out specifically what was going on with her cousin, but decided against it. Malik was his good friend. If something were bothering Carter, he would know and he would offer his help.

So instead of querying further about Carter, she'd shrugged, while Malik went back to mixing his oatmeal raisin cookie batter. He was trying out new recipes for the competition, using different ingredients, including Belgian chocolate, a delicious new French cream and a sweet and spicy Jamaican sugar. Each encompassed the Around the World theme but Malik needed to determine the best way to bring out their taste.

Belinda was silently grateful that this competition wasn't one of the ones that required them to use a mystery ingredient in a short amount of time. This way they had more than enough time for trial and error. Malik was dedicated to his work and, while not as obsessive as he considered her to be, Belinda knew he would spend the rest of the afternoon working through the trials and praying for no errors.

As for Shari, Belinda recalled their conversation of several days ago, before the dinner at Lillian's. Shari had been a little short with her. But Belinda hadn't thought too much of that since they'd had a lot of orders at the bakery, and then Shari had a child to go home and take care of. She figured it was just stress and decided it was best to leave her alone.

When Belinda had arrived at the bakery this morning, she'd hoped Shari would be in a better mood. She'd been wrong.

"So do you want to work on those two wedding cakes today while I do the Hassleman cupcakes?" Belinda had asked after she'd come in and retrieved her apron from the hook. Malik had hung his shirt for after work on the hook right beside hers. It had startled her when she saw

it, so much so she had to take a deep breath before saying anything. Then she'd touched it and thought of him,
of the nights they'd spent together at his place, no less.

She left the shirt where it hung.

"I've already started the cakes," was Shari's reply.

"Okay," she said, refusing to ask Shari any more
questions to which she'd no doubt receive an icy reply.
It wasn't worth the headache. If Shari wanted to talk,
she knew Belinda was there to listen, just as she'd always been. Maybe this was something her cousin would
have to go through on her own. Belinda certainly understood that.

Deciding against any further conversation, Belinda
set about making her cupcakes. Two hundred, not five
hundred like the dream she'd had a couple weeks ago.
Or rather the nightmare where she'd lost all control.
This morning she moved at a steady pace, doing things
she could probably do in her sleep. Her heart rate remained calm and she moved around with purpose but
not with anxiety.

The cupcakes were scheduled for a four o'clock
pickup. Belinda had them all baked, iced and packed by
2:45 p.m.—fifty double chocolate with hot pink frosting and two white sugar daisies on top; fifty vanilla
with light pink frosting and a hot pink candied bow on
top; fifty red velvet with white cream cheese icing and
tiny candied pink hearts on top; fifty lemon with white
icing and various shades of pink candied confetti on top.

It was now quarter to four and she had just taken
the last box out to the showroom so she wouldn't have
to run back and forth to get them when the customer
arrived.

"So I was thinking," Malik said, coming up behind

her and wrapping his arms around her waist. "How about we order in tonight and veg out in front of the television?"

Belinda smiled because she'd been thinking the same thing, at least about watching television.

"There's an *I Love Lucy* marathon on tonight," she told him, and laughed out loud when he groaned.

"Oh, come on, you know you love Lucy and Ricky." It was so easy to be with Malik, so relaxing and so comfortable. She often wondered why she hadn't tried this relationship thing before. Then knew without a doubt it wouldn't have worked with anyone else.

"I don't even remember Lucy and Ricky," Malik told her with a chuckle.

"We can watch a couple of episodes then it'll be your choice."

He turned her around in his arms and kissed the tip of her nose. "That's very big of you to compromise. So what do you want to eat? Chinese? Thai? Barbecue?"

"Mmmm, Chinese. Shrimp fried rice."

"No onions and no sprouts," he finished for her.

Again she smiled because Malik really did know her well.

"Isn't this cozy? Or it would be if you weren't in a place of business."

The sarcastic voice was like a splash of cold water.

"Hello, Mrs. Martin," Malik said, releasing Belinda from his hold and reluctantly going to the counter as he would for any customer.

Even though Chantelle Martin was not an ordinary customer.

"Hello, Malik. I see you apparently don't keep everyone at arm's length."

To his credit Malik didn't seem at all fazed by the tight pencil skirt Mrs. Martin wore today or the white blouse with rows of ruffles that sat even higher and puffier thanks to her voluptuous breasts.

"Is there something I can get for you today?" Malik asked.

She glanced Belinda's way and rolled her eyes. "I'm actually here to see her."

And the showdown would begin, Belinda thought as she stepped up to the counter.

"How can I help you?" The cordial tone and businesslike smile were second nature to Belinda. She wouldn't mind reverting back to her old ways of dealing with women like Mrs. Martin by having as sharp a tongue as her opponent.

"Not me. But you'll need to help yourself in a minute," was Chantelle's retort.

The door to the bakery opened once more and two uniformed officers walked inside.

"Belinda Drayson-Jones?" one of them asked, looking at Belinda.

Her heart had just begun to beat faster as Malik took a step closer to her.

"That's me," she replied.

The other officer came behind the counter and reached for her free hand.

"You have the right to remain silent," the first officer began.

Everything around her was spinning. Her heart beat so hard she thought it would thump right out of her chest. Malik was saying something as the officer took her other arm and secured the handcuffs on her.

She didn't know what he was saying, couldn't hear

anything beyond the rights the cop recited to her. Her vision was blurry but, as they moved her to the front door, she saw Chantelle Martin's face very clearly, the smirk of satisfaction too bright to ignore.

Chapter 17

Daisy and Matt Jones walked into the police department with an expensive-suit-wearing attorney right behind them. Malik knew things were about to get worse.

After the police had left the bakery with Belinda in tow, he'd immediately turned to Chantelle, rage simmering inside him.

"What the hell did you do? What did you tell them?" he asked her, trying like hell to keep from strangling her where she stood.

"Not all smiles and giggles now that you find out you're sleeping with a criminal, are you?" Chantelle asked, disdain clear in her voice.

"I'm not going to ask you nicely again, Chantelle. And I don't have time for your BS!" No, because he had to get to the police station and bail out his girlfriend.

By this time Carter and Shari had come from the

kitchen, probably wondering at the noise and commotion going on.

"Don't raise your voice at me. You should tell your girlfriend to stay in her lane. Kayla is my child, not hers. She had no business arranging some little meeting with her and convincing Kayla to run away. I'll bet she even knows where my child is."

"What the hell are you talking about? Belinda didn't kidnap anybody," Malik said, feeling like he was stuck in some alternate world where everything was ass backward and ridiculous.

"What?" Shari yelled from behind Malik. "Who is this woman and where is Belinda?"

Chantelle just nodded. "That's right, you're all family around here. Well, y'all better start selling more cupcakes and pies because bail money is not cheap. And if my daughter isn't found in the next twenty-four hours, I'm going to insist they charge her with kidnapping!"

Chantelle spun on her heel and nearly ran over the young couple picking up the cupcakes for their six-year-old twin girls' birthday party.

Malik hadn't stuck around to take care of the order. He'd run to the garage and climbed into his car. With his cell phone in hand he called his lawyer who, in turn, called a criminal defense lawyer. An hour later, when Malik sat in the lobby of the police station waiting for Belinda to be processed, Mitchell Panelos came in to talk with him.

"I don't care what it costs, just get her out of here," he told the lawyer.

With a nod Mitchell had clapped him on the shoulder and said, "Sit tight, I'll be right back."

He was still sitting tight when Daisy and her husband walked in.

"Find out who we need to speak to so my daughter can be released," she told the man who Malik assumed was an attorney.

He stood and walked the last few steps to them. "I've already hired an attorney and he's taking care of it."

Daisy looked over her shoulder at him as if he were a stranger. "Belinda is represented by Davenport & Gwin. Our entire family is," she told him.

Malik's first impression of Daisy had been that she was an overprotective mother of both her children. Then years passed and he realized there was more to her than just protecting her children. Daisy was trying to make up for the life she'd led. Not that she'd been a bad person, but Malik suspected she hadn't been the person she really wanted to be. She hadn't desired to be a baker like her mother had hoped, but housewife hadn't been her top pick, either. Yet that was how things had played out for her. Because of that sacrifice she felt Belinda and Drake, Belinda especially, owed it to her to do exactly as she advised, no matter what.

They'd been on cordial terms, but as she looked at Malik today, he knew that had changed the moment Belinda told her that they were together.

"I understand that," he told her. "But I hired Mitchell Panelos and he's already back there trying to get her released."

"There's no use for two attorneys," Matt interjected in his deep, gruff voice.

"But Davenport—"

"It doesn't make sense to have two attorneys, Daisy. Now, Malik's already hired an attorney for her who's working on getting her out. That's what we came to do. So since it's already done, let's just have a seat and wait."

"I want to know what's going on. Why was she arrested in the first place?" Daisy asked, switching gears.

"I trust Malik's going to fill us in on all the details," Matt said.

"And not a moment too soon," Drake added when he showed up, Carter and Shari right behind him.

So it was him against them. Not quite, he thought as he looked around. Daisy was the only one looking at him like she was ready to snap his neck.

"Chantelle Martin, that's the lady that was at the bakery. Belinda met her at my foundation's fund-raiser the week before last. Mrs. Martin is the parent of one of the boys who plays on my team. She apparently also has a daughter. I remember seeing Belinda talking to a girl that day. Then Belinda said she saw her again at the library a couple days after the event. Mrs. Martin made some crazy comments today about Belinda kidnapping her daughter or convincing her to run away from home."

"That's insane," Shari said.

"Right," Drake added. "It doesn't even sound right. First off, Belinda wouldn't go talk to some strange little girl. You know she has a thing about germs."

"Belinda did talk to Kayla at the fund-raiser," Malik countered. "She said she felt drawn to her since the little girl was alone, with no parents to watch her perform in the cheerleading competitions."

"But I thought you said Mrs. Martin was her mother and she was there," Carter interjected before Drake could make another statement.

"I didn't know Mrs. Martin had a daughter there.

I've never seen her with her daughter. But today she said Kayla was her daughter and I'm assuming Kayla has run away."

"Damn," Drake said. "This is not good."

"This is ridiculous," Shari said. "Belinda is not a kidnapper."

"I don't know what's been going through her head lately," Daisy said. "First the situation at my event and I had to smooth over things with the Mastersons after that. Now this. I don't know, Matt. Maybe she needs to see someone, talk to someone about what's going on with her."

"There's nothing going on with Belinda," Malik interrupted.

"Malik," Daisy started, "I know you two have gotten close over the years, but this is my daughter. I think I know when something's going on with her."

"With all due respect, ma'am, I'm telling you that nothing is going on with her. Belinda is just fine. In fact, she's better than fine," he said with conviction. He'd seen such a change in her the past few days. She was calmer, her brow not wrinkling so much as she tried to keep the control she was known for. She hadn't argued about staying at his place, even though she did make him move his sofa table closer to the door so she could set her purse there when she came in. And she'd dragged him to the store with her while she purchased feather-filled pillows like the one she had at her apartment, to place on the right side of his bed where she slept.

She was still Belinda, but she was different. She was evolving and he loved that about her.

"He's right, Aunt Daisy," Carter said, coming to stand beside Malik.

It was totally unnecessary. Malik didn't need any-body to back him up. He knew he was right about Be-linda and he wasn't the least bit concerned about how Daisy felt about them being together.

Still, it felt good and he silently looked over to Carter, giving him a nod of thanks.

"Belinda's doing well. She's been talking about plans for the competition and maybe taking some time off this summer. She's good," Carter told Daisy.

"She's in jail, Carter. Did you forget that little part of this scenario?" Daisy snapped. "That's not good!"

"Not for much longer," Mitchell Panelos said, com-ing to join the group.

"What happened? Is she getting out?" Shari was ask-ing, her shoulders sagging just a bit like she was the one now carrying the weight of the world.

"She's going to be released. There's no evidence against her. Nothing but the words of Mrs. Martin. The girl is still missing, but there's nothing to connect Belinda with that. Besides, she has alibis for when the girl went missing and a verified reason why she was at the library."

"Thanks, Mitchell," Malik said, reaching out a hand to shake the attorney's.

"No problem. And no charge," he told Malik with a nod. "But I'll be sending you the ball I received from one of your games for an autograph."

"You got it," Malik agreed with a smile.

The questions had gone on for what seemed like forever. All the while Belinda had sat with her back straight in a hard chair, staring at the officer who had handcuffed her, completely cooperating. The small room with its stale air was a little stifling and at one point she'd thought she might actually faint, but she'd reached for control and clasped her hands in her lap. All she had to do was answer their questions, tell the truth and this would all be over.

"So you haven't seen or spoken to Kayla Washington since that day at the library?" Officer Bent asked.

"That's correct," she said, her throat growing dry. "I met her at the rec center, the day of the fund-raiser. That was on a Sunday. That following Wednesday I went to the library to check on my schedule and she was there. We talked for maybe fifteen minutes. She asked about some books and I recommended a couple of new young adult releases. She left with her group leader and I stayed at the library another fifteen minutes speaking with the branch manager."

"And the first you heard of her running away was when?"

"When you told me," she replied.

The moment he'd said Kayla was missing Belinda had felt like a weight was crushing her chest. Her breathing had become labored and that's when she thought she would faint. Anxiety had crept up quickly, wrapping its ugly hands around her neck and holding it in a death grip. Until she'd pushed it away. It hadn't been easy, but necessary. Belinda had no idea where Kayla was and she certainly hadn't encouraged her to go in any way. Those were the facts and nobody could dispute them. Nobody with an ounce of sense, so Chantelle's allegations were just as off-kilter as the woman herself.

The episode had lasted less than five minutes. She'd blinked and focused until clarity was second nature and she'd told the officer what she knew. In the back of her mind she knew they couldn't hold her, couldn't charge her without some concrete proof. Still, sitting here under this interrogation was making her quite uneasy. When Mitchell Panelos walked into the room, introducing himself as her attorney, she'd felt nothing but relief.

"Thank you for coming down with us, Ms. Drayson-Jones."

She looked at the officer once more. "I didn't have much choice, did I?"

"A fact that I will be taking up with your superiors and quite possibly your legal department," Mr. Panelos told him in a no-nonsense voice.

He'd taken her by the arm and helped her up from the table. Officer Bent had taken a step back in defense, his cheeks turning ruby-red.

"We were simply following a lead. Mrs. Martin filed a complaint and we executed on it."

"You handcuffed her and brought her down here under the pretense that she was being charged," Panelos told him more vehemently.

"But we never charged her. I simply read her her rights. I didn't formally arrest her."

"She would have come in for questioning on her own if you'd just told her what you wanted. Dragging her out of her place of employment was unnecessary and most likely damaging," he continued to explain.

Belinda wasn't damaged. Or at least she was almost certain she wasn't. It was unpleasant and yes, unnecessary, but she wouldn't give Chantelle Martin the pleasure of damaging her in any way.

"We can just go now, right?" she prompted.

Officer Bent nodded quickly. "Yes. Yes, ma'am. You're free to leave."

He and Panelos exchanged a glare as they walked out of the room. Belinda didn't speak again until they were about to go through the double doors she knew led to the waiting room.

"Thank you," she said to Panelos, who was still holding on to her arm. "I don't know who hired you but I'll make sure you're compensated for your time."

"Your boyfriend hired me. But believe me, it was my pleasure. I've been buying my mother's birthday cake from Lillian's for ten years now."

When she looked up at him, he was smiling. A nice handsome smile that she was sure made some woman weak in the knees. As for her, each time Malik did something thoughtful for her, like hiring an attorney to get her out of jail, it wasn't weakness Belinda felt, but the strength of their love for each other.

That strength was about to be tested, she thought as she walked through the double doors to see her entire family waiting for her. Belinda didn't run to her mother, who had suddenly begun to tear up, or to her father, who looked toward her expectantly.

She walked straight into Malik's arms and held on to him just as tightly as he was holding on to her. It felt good right here, safe, not provoking or adding to an anxiety attack.

"All right, let's get you home," Daisy said from behind her.

The brisk tone of her mother's voice interrupted the calm Belinda had fought so hard for in the past few hours. Pulling away from Malik slightly, she could tell by the look on his face that he wanted to tell her mother to shut up. But he would never disrespect Daisy or any of her family members, she knew that for sure.

Belinda was all about respecting her family as well, as long as they respected her in return. Slowly she left his grasp and turned to face her parents. She went to her father because he'd always been a rock in her life, always listening to her every word, giving her all the love and support she could ever ask for. Wrapping her arms around him, she held on for a minute, inhaling his familiar scent. "I'm okay," she whispered to him.

When her father released her, she came up on tiptoe to plant a kiss on his bristly cheek. He smiled down at her and courage blossomed in her chest.

Then she moved to her mother and held her, as well.

"I'm going home with Malik," she said in no uncertain terms. "I will call you tomorrow."

Daisy, of course, disagreed. "Belinda, I am not going to stand here and—"

"Oh, shut up, Daisy," Grandma said, pushing her way between Daisy and Matt to get to Belinda.

Nobody knew she had arrived until she spoke. Now she came through the crowd like the force that she was.

She stepped right up to Belinda and put a hand on her cheek. "You all right?" she asked with great concern.

Belinda nodded. "I'm okay. It was a misunderstanding," she told them without going into more detail.

"Good. Go on home and get some rest. I don't want you in the bakery again until Monday," Lillian told her.

"But we have orders and Friday we were going to do a test run of some items for the competition," Belinda argued.

Lillian was already shaking her head. "No. You stay home and rest. We'll do the test run next week. You need to take some time for you. All this working and running around is stupid and you've been doing it for far too long."

Hallelujah, her heart sang. Someone else had finally said what she'd been afraid to believe. "You're right," Belinda said, and tried to ignore the surprised look on the faces of her family members. "I do need a break."

Drake looked like he wanted to say something else, but he quickly closed his mouth when Lillian shot him a searing glare. And when Malik reached for her hand, she eagerly accepted it. He led her through the crowd and she spied Carter making a "call me" signal to Malik as they left. Drake didn't look their way at all, but stood near his mother, his hand on her shoulder for support. It was Shari who stopped them to give Belinda a quick hug. "Glad you took my advice and snapped him up right quick," she said with a smile.

Belinda's answer was a smile in response. "So am I."

Chapter 18

They were going back to her place to pick up some clothes. Thanks to Lillian she'd be off for the rest of the week. During that time Belinda decided she would make it a point to visit with Shari and Andre at home. There was still something going on there, she saw it in Shari's eyes as she'd left the police station. And she would also work on some ideas from the competition. That was still a very important step in the history of Lillian's Bakery, one she was determined to play an integral—but not controlling—part in.

The ride across town had been quiet except for Malik's apology. The one she hadn't needed, but accepted anyway because it seemed so important to him.

"If I had put Chantelle in her place a long time ago, this would never have happened," he explained.

"I don't know if that's true. Some people are just too hardheaded for their own good." The words had made her smile but she'd noticed Malik still frowned. "I know you didn't mean for any of this to happen, and believe me, I don't think any of it was your fault. She's crazy, not you. Or me, for that matter. Besides, it's over. We can get on with our lives now."

She lifted a hand to cup his cheek.

"Is that what you want? To get on with our lives?" he asked in a hoarse whisper.

Leaning forward, she kissed his lips lightly. "That's exactly what I want."

After the car was parked and they'd taken the elevator up to her floor, Malik used the keys she'd already given him and moved to unlock the door. When he touched the doorknob, it turned because it was already unlocked.

He immediately extended an arm out in front of her, pushing her back. "Get your cell and dial 9-1-1," he told her.

"Don't go in there," she was saying as she rooted around in her purse for her phone.

Malik ignored her. He was already heading into the apartment.

At first glance Belinda didn't see anything out of place and it looked as if all her stuff was there. The plasma television was still bolted to the wall; the few bronze pieces were still on the stand where she kept them. Malik paused a second to pick one up, holding it in his hand like a weapon and proceeded into the dining room. She followed behind him.

"It's my apartment, Malik. I know you didn't think I was going to wait outside."

She had her arms folded tightly around herself.

Knowing damned well that's what he'd intended for her to do.

"Don't touch anything," she told him, ignoring the fact that he looked at her strangely.

"I'm not going to touch," he said, then stopped when they both heard glass breaking in the kitchen.

"Stay here," he told her specifically this time.

But the minute he'd pushed through the swinging kitchen door and paused suddenly, Belinda slammed against his back. Malik didn't even turn around.

"What the hell?" he said as they spotted the young girl kneeling down and picking up pieces of shattered glass off the floor.

"You scared me and I dropped it," she said in defense, her big brown eyes etched with fear.

Belinda came from behind him. "Kayla? What are you doing here?"

Kayla stood, going to the trash can with as much familiarity as if she lived here. "You said if I needed you, you'd be here. When I showed up last night, I knocked and knocked, but you weren't here."

"So you broke in?" Malik asked, crossing the room to where she'd been and kneeling to pick up the rest of the glass.

"I didn't have anywhere else to go," she said slowly. "Are you mad at me?"

"Of course I'm not mad, Kayla." Belinda had moved also and was now pulling Kayla close for a hug. "But all you had to do was call me. I would have come and picked you up."

Hearing herself say those words, Belinda knew she would have done just that. It didn't matter to her that this child had a mother and possibly a father someplace.

If Kayla had reached out in need, Belinda would have been there to supply it. It was as simple as that.

"But you do have some explaining to do," she told her. "And we have to clean up this mess." Because it was already working on Belinda's nerves.

Obviously the little girl was hungry because she'd gone through all the cabinets looking for something she could fix to eat. It looked like she'd settled on a peanut butter and jelly sandwich.

She began passing Kayla things to put away while Malik retrieved the broom and dustpan from the slim utility closet near the door and swept the remaining glass off the floor.

"Why did you run away?" Belinda asked while they moved, trying to keep the scene as calm as she could, keeping in mind she'd already called 9-1-1 and the police would be here momentarily.

"She doesn't care about me. All she worries about is Jarrod and Jaylen. She buys them everything for basketball, just everything. But when I ask for something, she tells me she doesn't have any money and I need to start helping out around the house. That's all she wants me to do—clean and cook and act like the mother. I'm not the mother!" Kayla said vehemently.

Belinda held open the dishwasher as Kayla lined the plate and the utensils she'd used in the appropriate slots. Closing the door and pushing the settings, Belinda felt her heart breaking for this child.

"You're not the mother," she told Kayla. "But you are just a child. Running away was wrong. You worried a lot of people."

"I'm sorry if I worried you," Kayla said earnestly. "But she doesn't care. All she cares about is the check she gets because my father was killed. If I'm not living with her, she doesn't get that check anymore."

"She gets a social security check for you?" Malik asked.

Kayla nodded. Her ponytail was a lot messier than it had been at the rec center and she was wearing faded capri jeans and a white shirt with some sort of cartoon character on the front. She was only fourteen, Belinda thought with a pang of sadness. Fourteen and wandering around the streets of Chicago on her own because she didn't think her mother wanted her. It was a shame.

"You know we have to take you back," Malik continued as he'd moved to stand on the other side of Kayla.

"But why can't I just stay here with you?"

She looked up at Belinda so imploringly and Belinda wanted to wrap her arms around her again and tell her she could. She wanted to keep this little girl and raise her as her own. Her heart pounded in her chest, this time not with anxiety, but with emotion that she couldn't quite explain.

"I can't, Kayla." When the girl looked away like she didn't want Belinda to see her cry, Belinda touched a hand to her cheek and turned her back to face her. "Not because I don't want to, because I do. You have no idea how much I'd love to bring you to live with me and raise you as my own. But that's not how the world works."

"If she doesn't want me, then I don't want her!" Kayla said defiantly.

"Why do you think she doesn't want you?" Belinda asked because the thought of a parent not wanting their child was mind-boggling to her. Even Daisy wanted Belinda, in her own crazy way.

"Because I'm a girl. Only the boys have potential,

because they can play for the NBA and make a lot of money for her to live like she wants. I'm good at cheer-leading and I'm cute but that's only going to get me into a good high school then I'll have to survive on my back. That's what she said."

That bitch! Belinda had to clench her teeth to keep from saying that aloud.

"That's not true," Malik interjected. "They have college scholarships for cheerleading, too."

Kayla shook her head. "But I don't want to be a cheerleader all my life. I want to be a teacher."

Belinda now knew how it felt to be loved. When she looked over at Malik and he gave her an understand-ing glance, her heart was so full. Unfortunately, at the same time she also knew how it felt for one's heart to break with sadness. Kayla was her, in a different set-ting, in different circumstances. She was the little girl who wanted to be herself but was constrained by her mother's hand. Belinda struggled to fight back tears.

The police arrived in the next few minutes and Malik went to talk with them while Belinda held a quietly cry-ing Kayla in her arms.

At a little after midnight Malik and Belinda were leaving the police department for the second time in a twenty-four-hour time span. Mrs. Martin had been called to come pick up Kayla, but by Belinda's insis-tence and her threat to sue the whole police department for her false arrest, she had them contact the Depart-ment of Social Services, as well. If she couldn't take Kayla home with her, she wanted to know the little girl was at least going to have someone she could talk to about what she was going through.

"You stay the hell away from my child!" Mrs. Martin

screamed as she saw Belinda leaving the room where they were holding Kayla. "And I'm taking my son off your team. Coach Sanders has other plans for him. Bigger plans than you could ever imagine," she spat at Malik.

"Come on, baby," he said, putting his arm around Belinda's shoulders and escorting her away. "You can't save everybody."

Belinda walked beside him, resting her head on his shoulder. "Not everybody, Malik. Just her. I just want to save Kayla."

An hour later they were back at Malik's apartment, his whirlpool tub full of hot water as they both sank their tired bodies into the waiting bliss.

This was another first for her but Belinda was loving the feel of sitting between Malik's legs, laying her naked body back against his. He wrapped his arms around her, hugging her tightly.

"It's been a long night."

"A very long night," she agreed.

"You were good, though. Strong and composed. I was very proud of you."

"I was scared to death. I've never been handcuffed and taken to a police station before," she admitted.

"I was scared to death." He echoed her sentiments. "I've never had to watch someone I love be handcuffed and taken to a police station before."

"You were my hero. You came to get me," she said, rubbing her hands along his now wet arms. She loved the strength of his arms, the safety she felt there. Malik would protect her no matter what. He would stand up to idiots like Patrick Masterson as well as the loving ignorance of her mother. He didn't care that she was a little on the obsessive side—she could admit that without thinking herself crazy. And he didn't care that she would sometimes be unyielding. He loved her just as she was.

"I would go to the ends of this earth for you, baby."

And he meant that. Belinda knew without a doubt he meant every word.

"I'm so glad I decided to change and that you were there to help me. I'm so happy to be with you and to know you love me, because I love you right back," she told him honestly, her heart overflowing with love.

She looked back at him to see him smiling down at her. Then his eyes darkened and he lowered his head to kiss her lips. His tongue moved languidly over hers, their arousal growing as hot as the water they sat in.

"I have a very important question for you, Belinda Drayson-Jones," he said as he pulled back slightly, rubbing his nose along hers.

Belinda held her breath then thought she'd better let it out. It wouldn't do for her to receive her first wedding proposal then pass out from lack of oxygen seconds later.

"Yes," she replied in a breathy whisper.

"You ever made love in a whirlpool before?"

"No," was her answer, followed by a sigh when his lips touched hers again. She should probably feel disappointed because that wasn't the question she was expecting to hear, but as Malik's hands moved lower, her breathing spiked along with her body temperature. By then the question didn't matter, only the sensations, the emotions, the feel of his love as he turned her to face him and sank deep inside her. It was truly decadent, this feeling of complete love and satisfaction, and better than any dream she'd ever had.

* * * * *

REQUEST YOUR FREE BOOKS!

2 FREE NOVELS
PLUS 2 *FREE GIFTS!*

KIMANI™ ROMANCE

Love's ultimate destination!